Dead Flowers Baited

Lori Armstrong

COPYRIGHT PAGE

Dead Flowers*
Lori Armstrong
Published by LJLA, LLC

Edited by Charlotte Herscher
Original digital cover by Shawn Gross Photography
*previously digitally published in Guns And Roses Anthology 2012

BAITED
Lori Armstrong
Published by LJLA, LLC

Edited by: Valerie Gray/EditABook
Original digital cover by: The Cover Collection
Print ISBN: 978-0-9888235-6-3

Print cover by Meredith Blair
www.authorsangels.com

Dead Flowers

A Julie Collins novella

I fucking hated Valentine's Day.

Hated it.

With the hatred of a thousand fiery suns kind of hatred.

"Yes, Julie, I know. You've been bitching about it for the last three days. Give it a rest."

I glanced across the conference table at my PI partner in crime, Kevin Wells.

"What?" His handsome face wore a mocking expression. "No, I'm not a mind reader. You're muttering. But in your case, it's not really muttering, since I can understand every snarky word."

"So you're a fan of Valentine's Day? You're picking out a mushy card, a box of chocolates, a bunch of flowers, and a teddy bear... for who exactly?"

"No one, and I'm damn happy not to be dropping a bundle on one day without the guarantee I'll get laid. Beings you're in *lurve* and all, I imagine you're planning to don fetish wear for Martinez for Valentine's Day."

I gave him a droll stare. "Really, Kev? Fetish wear?"

"I thought all bikers were into latex, leather and chains, and kinky stuff. I expect Martinez is the type of man to demand you put it on and parade around for his pleasure."

"Demand? That'd be the first and last time. I'd kick his ass."

"Sure. And then you'd kiss it."

My blood pressure spiked when he made kissing noises. "What the fuck is *wrong* with you today?"

Kevin grinned. "I love yanking your chain. Especially the one Martinez used to attach the ball around your ankle. I'm surprised it doesn't trip you up more often."

I threw the stapler at him.

He ducked, laughed, then hightailed it out to the main room when the doorbell dinged.

My whole beef with Valentine's Day, at least this year, was that we, at Wells/Collins Investigations, had spent the last month working on cases to verify infidelity. Following the suspect-ees, hoping to catch them in trysts. The worst ones? When the cheaters were bold enough to meet their no-tell lover in their own homes. For me, it was enough to tarnish the aspect of everlasting love. It made me loathe a day devoted to celebrating lovers.

Wasn't like Martinez and I had discussed V-day. Not even in the hope-you-aren't-expecting-an-engagement-ring type of joking around. Martinez and I had been living together for almost a year. The blush wasn't entirely off the rose, but the petals had started to droop, especially since the first of the year. He'd been distant, which I chalked up to Hombres problems, not anything going wrong between us.

Or had I just gotten complacent?

I knew better than to ask why Martinez always left the room when his private cell phone rang. Secrecy was part of the gig being involved with Tony Martinez, the international president of the Hombres motorcycle club. Part of me was happy he kept me in the dark about his shady business dealings. But another part of me wondered if that mentality made me as much an idiot as the clients who hired us, hopeful the suspicions about their lover's indiscretions were wrong. After all Tony and I had gone through to be together, he wouldn't be stepping out on me now... would he?

It especially bugged me, that in the last two months, more often than not, he still crashed at Bare Assets, the strip club he owned, or Fat Bob's, the biker bar he owned, rather than driving home.

Home. Even after eight months, it sounded strange. The place still felt like I was living in a hotel. We'd done nothing to it to make it ours besides combining our various crappy personal belongings.

After I'd sold my house in Bear Butte County, he'd found a duplex to suit our needs. The house is located out of town, past the airport, and situated on a hill. Which means we have a great view of the front side of the Black Hills of South Dakota and the backside of the Badlands. We're surrounded by ag land, so no one can show up on our doorstep and get to El Presidente without tipping off his security team.

"Julie? We have a visitor."

I looked up as Kevin entered the conference room with a smartly dressed brunette. The woman, I guessed in her late-fifties, pointedly stepped over the stapler on the floor, offering her gloved hand and a brittle smile. "Marcia Bueller."

"Julie Collins." I studied her for a moment. "Bueller. As in the Bueller Law Office down the hall from us?"

"One and the same. My husband, Glen Bueller, owns the firm. I know he hasn't utilized your investigative services, despite the convenience."

Kevin and I exchanged a look. Glen Bueller had leased the small office space six months ago. It'd seemed odd that the lawyer, who looked maybe five years shy of retirement, had left a large prestigious firm to hang out his own legal shingle at the twilight of his career.

"Why don't you tell us what problem we'll be assisting you with?" Kevin said.

Gotta love my smooth partner and his optimism.

A long minute passed before she offered, "It's a... personal matter."

Kevin's attention remained rapt. Mine wandered. I hated how some clients dragged out the drama. Wouldn't make the case more interesting to me. Nothing piqued my interest like cash on the barrelhead.

"Two years ago, Glen took on a junior associate. A young woman, fresh out of law school, who'd spent a year clerking for Judge Raba in seventh circuit district court. When my husband relinquished his partnership last year, Meghan opted to join him in his solo practice."

I'd seen this Meghan woman. A tall, stacked, gorgeous redhead who could've moonlighted as the main attraction at Martinez' strip club. "Didn't you object to him hiring her?"

Marcia shook her head. "I encouraged him to hire her since Meghan is the daughter of my sorority sister, Patrice. I expected it'd be a mentor relationship. Then he had a career crisis and resigned from Hall, Nelsen, and Burns to start his own practice. He didn't consult me in that decision."

"It's caused issues between you?"

"Yes, not that I ever expressed my displeasure to him. I soldiered on, being the dutiful wife as I have for the last thirty-five years. But now..." Marcia glanced at her gloved hands, folded on the conference table. "Now I'm afraid they're having an affair."

"What makes you believe that?" Kevin asked.

"Little things. The familiar way she touches him. The avidness of his eyes following her every move. The last minute business trips. The fact that when he's home, he's not... really there. He's distracted."

Don't compare this situation to yours with Martinez.

Annoyed by my own comparison, I asked, "When did you first suspect this was going on?"

Marcia lifted her chin, glared at me for my impertinent question and then addressed Kevin. "I need to know exactly what's going on. Irrefutable proof. I assume you can be discreet?"

"Absolutely."

"Then I'd like to hire you."

"Consider it done." Kevin leveled her with a *trust me I'm a professional smile.* "Hang tight for a second and I'll get the paperwork."

I sensed Marcia didn't want to be alone with me because I'd already figured out she'd known about her husband's slap and tickle with his associate a lot longer than she wanted to admit.

So what'd happened all of a sudden that she could open the blind eye she'd turned toward the affair? Despite my usual tendency to blurt out the first thing that popped into my head, this time, I kept my mouth shut and put the business ahead of my curiosity.

I fired up a smoke and leaned back in my chair.

Marcia wrinkled her nose. "There are no smoking laws in this city."

"Would you like me to open a window?" Right. It was ten degrees below zero outside.

"I'm sure the building owners wouldn't approve of your... habit."

"Moot point since Kevin now owns the building." Technically Kevin, Jimmer and I owned it. Jimmer needed a legitimate tax write off, and I needed to invest the paltry sum from the sale of my house since Martinez had paid for ours. And luckily, my buddy Kevin oozed the charm that'd convinced the ninety-something spitfire Verna Doren to sell to us two months ago. I exhaled. Smiled. Waited.

"You and Kevin are partners?"

So damn hard not to snipe back that Kevin and I weren't partners like her husband and Meghan were partners. "Yes. Kevin started the business, but I bought in after I quit working at the Bear Butte County Sheriff's Office a few years ago."

Kevin returned with the contract. I listened while he explained the terms. Marcia signed on the dotted line and they left to take care of payment. Cash I assumed.

I ground out my smoke and wandered to the window, looking at the street below. Dirty snow was piled waist high against the stone façade. A Dumpster in the alley overflowed with cardboard. The dim sunlight was fading fast, tipping us into night. I'd be glad to put this day behind me and go home.

Would Martinez be there tonight? Or would I get another terse phone call telling me not to wait up? I brooded until Kevin returned.

"Jules? You okay?"

"Yeah." I faced him. "Just ready to be done with these cases today."

Kevin slid into his seat. "Speaking of cases... what have we got on Natalie Brunson, besides her husband's suspicion that she's getting it on with their son's math tutor?"

"Photos." I shoved the pictures at him. "They meet every other day in the morning."

"Think math whiz college kid has calculated how much each bang is worth?"

"Crude, even for you, Kev. Besides"—I tapped my fingers on the pictures—"I don't know how damning these are."

"What's the time between shots?" Kevin asked.

"Forty-five minutes. After the meeting, they lingered on the doorstep, as much as one can linger when it's three degrees below zero out. They didn't touch at all, which could be an indication they're doing the nasty. Or it could be... they're simply an employer/employee chatting about the kid's performance, not how the tutor performs in bed."

Kevin squinted at me. Then he bent down and peeked under the table.

"Did you lose your pen or something?"

He raised his head. "I see you. I hear your voice, but the excuses you're offering would never come out of my cynical partner's mouth. Never."

"Good one, Shecky."

"Seriously, you've been *all these assholes are fucking cheaters* and now you're changing your tune? Because she's a woman and women don't cheat?"

"No. And fuck off for assuming I'm gender biased when it comes to cheating. When I saw them on the steps, it wasn't lovers saying goodbye. It was more like... when you walk a friend out the front door and your conversation lingers."

"Does that happen when your BFF, Kim, and her new bundle of joy comes over to the place you share with Martinez?"

I shuffled the pictures, a little pissy he'd touched on another sore subject between me and Martinez. The "no visitors" rule. "Kim doesn't visit me. Guns, goons and babies don't mix. Even if she did visit, one of Martinez' bodyguards would warn her off with a shotgun."

"How can you live like that?"

"I'm used to it." The threats to Martinez had lessened in the last year, but hadn't disappeared completely. So a rotating security detail of seven club members protected us 24/7, two guys for two days at a time. Martinez and I occupy one side of the duplex and his security team the other. A door connects the two separate spaces. A door, which is never locked from our side. That main door has to be 100% accessible 100% of the time for Martinez' protection.

"You put up with a lot of shit to live with him, Jules. You know that, right?"

I shrugged. "My other choice is not to live with him at all." That I couldn't handle. "As far as Natalie Brunson... I'll need another day. Three hours remain on the husband's initial payment anyway."

Kevin made a disgruntled sigh. "Immediately after you're done tomorrow, do the wrap-up report so I can call him."

"Happy fucking Valentine's Day." I gathered the pictures and dropped them in the manila envelope. "You're handling Marcia Bueller's case?"

"Yes. But I felt guilty taking her money. I already know Meghan is frequently in old man Bueller briefs—not just the legal ones."

"How?"

His cool green-eyed stare tightened my midsection. "Paper-thin walls. I've heard them going at it on numerous occasions when I've worked late. I saw them playing grab ass in the hallway just last week."

My fist hit the conference table. "Why didn't you just tell Marcia that?"

"She wants tangible proof of her suspicions, so we'll give it to her." He sighed again. "Looks like I'm on stakeout duty tonight. Marcia said Glen planned to work late and told her not to wait up."

Just what Martinez had said to me the last few nights. Any desire to go home evaporated. "I can stay and help."

Kevin's gaze snapped to mine. "I thought you were antsy to leave and play kissy face with your man?"

Given my mood, I'd most likely punch Martinez in the kisser if I saw him. "And miss a chance to hear the old guy and the young tart squeaking the legs on the conference table? I'll stick around just to make Viagra jokes."

"Oh joy, my night will be complete."

"Want me to order pizza or Chinese for stakeout duty?"

"Pizza. Veggie pizza. And get a salad with it."

Despite Kevin's resolution to become Mr. Health Conscious since New Years, I knew he'd eat his fair share of the chocolate marshmallow dessert pizza I planned to wallow in, since tequila wasn't an option while I was on duty.

~*~

As far as stakeouts? Our agency hit a new record for efficiency. I was able to sneak into the Bueller Law Office and record the sounds of skin slapping, grunts, and shouts of ecstasy, after I convinced the pizza delivery guy to accidentally deliver the order to the wrong office. For an extra twenty bucks, he'd been more than happy to leave the door open a crack.

Then Kevin had waited in a dark corner to snap photos with his super-duper, secret-spy camera of the pair swapping spit at the office doorway. Then Mr. Bueller took his cheating self down the back staircase while Meghan sashayed out the front door. Really. Who did they think they were fooling?

Kevin sensed my melancholy and offered to buy me a drink at the brewpub down the street from our office, but I declined and headed to the parking lot.

The digital thermometer in my pickup read the outside air temp as eighteen degrees. Below zero. As I waited for the engine to warm up, I smoked and considered my options. Pop in and visit Martinez unannounced? Just drive past Bare Assets and Fat Bob's looking for one of Martinez' four vehicles? No. That'd be creepy, girlfriend stalkerish. If he wanted me to know where he was, he'd tell me. I'd be damned if I'd call and check up on him.

Or maybe he thinks you don't give a shit.

Wrong. He knew how I felt about him. I wasn't the one who needed to prove those feelings hadn't faded since we'd moved in together.

The roads out of town were snow-packed and slippery. Ghostly white fingers skittered on the road in front of me, compelling in their haunting beauty. I slowed when I passed Black Hills Speedway and saw a car in the ditch. My Ford looked like a bucket of bolts on the outside, but the sucker got around like a mountain goat in the winter months. I ground out my second smoke right before I hit the turnoff to our place.

No gate. No outwardly obvious security measures. But hidden cameras monitored the entire area. The half-mile long gravel road leading to the house looked like just another untended country driveway—one of hundreds scattered across western South Dakota. I pulled around back and parked in the garage.

Buzz and Bucket were on duty. I punched the all clear code and let myself in.

The living room remained in the same messy state as this morning. My half-empty coffee cup on the end table next to an overflowing ashtray. Magazines scattered everywhere. A psychedelic-colored fleece blanket hung off the easy chair. Slippers and socks kicked off here and there. Martinez hated clutter. If he'd been around, he would've picked it up. Petty, but I'd left it that way for that reason.

I ditched my work clothes and slipped on my rattiest flannel pajamas. After fixing myself a bag of microwave popcorn, I snuggled into the leather couch and watched a *Myth Busters* marathon until sleep overtook me.

Cold air violated my warm cocoon and I protested until a pair of strong arms scooped me up. Although I was only groggy, I feigned sleep. What delicious way would Tony awaken me? I was hoping for hot skin, hot kisses and hot man all over me. Thickly whispered Spanish phrases in my ear as he slammed his body into mine. I could almost taste his full lips. I could almost feel his heart thundering against my chest as we tried to outdo each other, tried to push the other to the pinnacle of pleasure first. I could almost feel those clever, rough-skinned hands caressing my skin. Soothing me in the aftermath of volatile sex that left me breathless and more in love and in tune with him than before.

But as it turned out, Tony had nothing planned. He tucked me in. Stroked my hair. Kissed my cheek. My forehead. My temple. Between my eyebrows. He nuzzled my neck. He breathed me in and sighed.

This close, I detected another scent under that familiar tang of leather and his pine-scented soap. Something... sweet. Perfume. Subtle, but there. Not my brand since I didn't wear perfume.

My pretense of faking sleep vanished. When Tony eased back to smooth my hair from my face, he was surprised to see my eyes were open. And hard as ice.

"Don't give me the death glare, blondie. I didn't mean to wake you."

"Then you should've left me sleeping on the couch." I eyed him, the handsome fucker, from the midnight black hair brushing the collar of his leather jacket, down his jeans to his biker boots. "I see you're still in your outerwear which means you're not staying even though it's"—I glanced at the alarm clock—"four o'clock in the morning."

"I needed a change of clothes." He kept his back to me as he rooted in his dresser drawers.

"You going out of town?"

"No."

"You moving out?"

Tony stiffened. He turned toward me very slowly. Even in the darkness, I knew his eyes had gone flat and cold. "Why would you ask that?"

"Because you haven't been here and when you are, you're not really here." I stood because I refused to have this conversation lying down.

He didn't say anything. I couldn't read him, and that scared me. And as usual, I was the one who broke the mind-fuck eye lock first.

But I didn't back down entirely. "Who is she, Martinez?"

"Who is who?"

"The woman whose perfume is all over you." The look on his face indicated I'd actually shocked him.

"You think I'm cheating on you?"

"Are you?"

Martinez slammed the dresser drawer shut and shoved his clothes into his duffel bag. Then he shouldered it and looked at me. "I won't dignify that with a response, and I'm more than a little pissed off you even asked."

But he wasn't denying it.

Goddamn him. I wanted to throw something. Wanted to scream and rage. But I didn't. I played it as cool and aloof as he did.

He stopped at the door. Seemed about to say something. But he shook his head and walked out.

And I let him.

~*~

Despite my exhaustion—I hadn't slept more than twenty minutes after Tony left—I made it to my stakeout spot across the street from the Brunson's. Part of me hoped the math tutor wouldn't show today.

My wishful thinking was short lived.

The tutor parked in the driveway and left the engine running. Natalie Brunson climbed in the passenger side of the beat up Impala.

This was a new development.

I zoomed in with my camera, expecting a kiss or a show of affection, but nothing. Was I disappointed? Or relieved? With an hour still allotted on the client's dime, I followed them.

They pulled into the strip mall on Omaha Street and headed into Dunn Brothers coffee shop.

I parked at the far end by Pauly's Sub Shop and browsed at the other storefronts before I wandered in. The place wasn't busy and Natalie and the tutor had already claimed a booth across from the pastry case. In my mind, if they had something to hide, they would've taken a table in the back room. I ordered a cup of black coffee, scowled at the pink and red cupcakes with a plastic Cupid on the top, purchased a copy of the Rapid City Journal, and slid into the booth in front of them, keeping my back to the door.

Normally, I didn't perform surveillance close enough to warrant a disguise, but today I'd slipped on an army green Moosejaw knit cap and kept my scarf wrapped around my neck, so I could hide the lower half of my face if need be. The way I wore the cap made me look like Dopey from *Snow White* but I had to keep my ears uncovered so I could hear.

I tuned out all noises but their conversation behind me.

"What are you saying?" Natalie asked the tutor. "My son doesn't give a crap about calculus?"

"Look, I can help Braden get a passing grade in the class, if that's all you and Mr. Brunson want. But if your husband's expectations are that my teaching methods will make Braden love math and want to become an engineer like him... then I'll have to quit working with him."

"We've talked about why I need you to continue."

The tutor sighed. "I don't want that burden, either. I thought I could do this, Mrs. B, but I can't. And to be honest, Braden is starting to... suspect."

"Why?"

"He asked me last night why you and I meet so much."

Neither said anything else and I sipped my coffee, feigning interest in the letters to the editor.

That's when I heard the laugh. The warm, deep laugh that rolled over my skin like a velvet caress.

What was Martinez doing in here?

Granted, this coffee shop was closest to the strip club, but he usually sent a minion for his morning caffeine fix.

And why the hell was he laughing? He should be moping we'd had a fight, just like I was.

I remained statue-still, sharpening my auditory focus to the timbre of his voice. A woman responded to his query about a scone with a flirty comment, dripping with sexual innuendo.

Don't turn around. Don't jump to conclusions. Gather the facts first.

Martinez' order included three scones, two large coffees and one chai hot tea, which meant Big Mike was with them.

I was in limbo, unable to give away my position because I was on a case. But I couldn't focus on my job because I was too focused on my lover sharing coffee and laughs with another woman right under my nose.

Natalie and the tutor made preparations to leave. I did too, as discreetly as possible. I ducked into the back room, but my pride demanded I poke my head around the corner for a look. I saw Martinez and his entourage in the conversation area by the front doors. Tony leaned forward, listening intently to the brunette who had her back to me.

Lingering wasn't an option and somehow, I tamped down my jealousy as I booked it out the back door.

I disobeyed several traffic laws getting into place on Natalie's street. The tutor dropped her off and his car belched blue smoke as he cruised out of sight. I'd give the client the full ten minutes owed before I headed to the office.

Five minutes later two taps on my window startled me. I turned and looked into Natalie Brunson's face.

Shit. Busted. I rolled down the window and said brightly, "Yes?"

"This is the third time I've seen you on our street. And you were just in the coffee shop."

So much for my disguise.

"My husband hired you, didn't he?"

No accusation in the tone, which was odd. Other times I'd gotten busted doing surveillance, the person had been infuriated, lashing out at me for capturing proof of their infidelity. "Yes, he did."

"Can I talk to you about it?"

"Sure. Hop in. But understand I am armed and my partner is aware of my whereabouts."

Undeterred by my threat, Natalie Brunson climbed in the passenger's side. After seeing the ashtray overflowing with cigarette butts, she took out a pack of Newports and lit up.

I sparked a Marlboro. Maybe she thought we'd bond over our mutual bad habit.

After a couple of puffs, she said, "Once a cheater, always a cheater, right?"

She wasn't our client and I owed her nothing. But listening wouldn't hurt.

"Here's the lowdown on why Tad hired you. Ten years ago, I stupidly had an affair. First and only time I've ever lapsed in my marriage vows. The guilt ate at me and I confessed that lapse to Tad. We went through counseling and I thought we were okay... But the next year when Tad hired a painter—a male painter—to spruce up the outside of our house, I had that eerie feeling someone was watching me. Long story short, I discovered he'd hired a security specialist to keep tabs on my interaction with the painter. Every couple years something trips him offline and he gets a bug up his ass that I'm having an affair again." She exhaled a long stream of smoke. "So he's convinced I'm doing the deed with our son's math tutor."

I flicked an ash and waited for the excuses.

"That's almost funny. Even if you've been peeking in the windows, you'd know I'm not sleeping with Steven. But because *I* hired Steven and wouldn't consider any of Tad's tutor recommendations, I'm under suspicion." She drew in another hit of nicotine. "Seems I'll always be under suspicion."

"Why put up with that?" Hadn't Kevin said the same thing to me about Martinez?

"I'm wondering that myself." She put out her cigarette. "Tell him I'm fucking the kid blind. That lie will be easier for him than knowing the truth."

"What truth?" I said automatically.

Natalie expelled a harsh laugh. "Huh-uh. I know how this goes. Tad hired you. Your loyalty is to him."

I shrugged. "Technically, I'm off the clock as of"—I glanced at the digital display—"two minutes ago. Whatever you say stays between us." And my curiosity was definitely getting the better of me.

She gave me a peculiar look. "Why would you care?"

"I'm nosy. It's why I make a good PI."

Another laugh. Then her face sobered. "The truth is our son, Braden, came out to me six months ago. He's been struggling in all aspects of his life, not just his grades. Tad won't accept Braden being gay any more than he'll accept that Braden hates math and doesn't want to be an engineer. I hired Steven not only to get Braden's grades back up, but because Steven is gay."

That seemed convenient. "How did you know Steven is gay?"

"Steven's mother and I worked together a few years ago. Until Tad put my boss under surveillance because he was convinced we were going at it in the stockroom."

"That's... hard core suspicion."

"I lost that job because of Tad's paranoia. Again, I don't know why I put up with it. I made one mistake. A decade ago. Tad won't ever forget it."

Could I forgive and forget if the same were true of Martinez?

"Steven's in grad school at the School of Mines and offers tutoring. I thought it'd be easier for Braden to talk to Steven about being gay as he brought his grades up to snuff."

"I'm sorry you're forced to lie to your husband to protect your son."

"But?"

"But I won't lie to our client. My report will state that you aren't having an affair."

A minute or so of silence passed. "The truth doesn't always set you free, does it?" She exited the cab, leaving me staring after her.

I drove to the office. No sign of Kevin. Armed with coffee, I forced myself to finish the Brunson report. When I reached the part about following them to the coffee shop, my fingers hesitated on the keyboard.

Was I overreacting about Martinez having coffee with another woman? Should I apply the same logic to my own situation? That his public meeting with her and Big Mike meant he wasn't doing anything wrong and didn't have anything to hide?

Or maybe he didn't care if I found out.

On impulse, I called Big Mike.

"Yo, Julie, what's up?"

"Not much. I know bossman is busy so I'll ask you a quick question."

"Shoot."

"Did you guys send a couple cars by the office today? I saw two Navigators pull up across the street, but no one ever got out. I wondered if Tony had gotten called away suddenly or something before he could pop in for a visit."

"When was this?"

"Around nine."

"Nope. Couldn't have been us. We've been in meetings at Fat Bob's since the crack of dawn this morning."

Such a liar.

"Do you think someone is following you?" he asked sharply.

"No. But you oughta put markings on your cars so I can tell them apart from the other thug vehicles. Like a big letter A in the back window." I doubted Big Mike would get the reference.

He laughed. "And the A stands for...?"

"Asshole." I hung up.

I don't know how long I stared into space. Cross, miserable, remorseful—which was just fucking stupid since I wasn't the goddamned one at fault. The truth was beating at me from all sides... lies, evasion, absence. So why was I still in denial?

I'd just clamped a Marlboro between my lips when the door blew open, courtesy of my buddy, Jimmer Cheadle. At six feet six inches tall and wide as a Peterbilt truck, Jimmer wasn't exactly docile.

He scowled at my unlit cigarette. "I thought you were quitting that nasty habit as a New Year's resolution."

"Nope. Did you get hired by the resolution police to crack down on repeat offenders?"

"Funny." A smirk settled on his mouth as he plopped in the buffalo skin chair across from me, propping his size-twenty feet on my desk. "I just figured now that you and Tony have been shacked up for almost a year, you'd be hankering to hear the pitter patter of little feet. Sucking on a cancer stick is a no-no, little missy. That kid'll have three eyes."

I flicked my bejeweled Zippo lighter—a gift from Martinez. "I already hear the pitter patter of Martinez' bodyguards feet. Constantly." I inhaled. Exhaled. "Besides, if I want to subject myself to pooping, barfing, and screaming, I can get it from Kim's precious babe, Abby. I'm cool with not smoking around her little baby lungs, but I hate that Kim and Murray make me bathe in hand sanitizer before I can even poke her jelly belly."

"I hear ya. Know what I hate? When the first question outta my date's mouth is if I want kids."

I tried to wrap my head around Jimmer dating. I must've had a funny look on my face because Jimmer said, "What?"

"Just envisioning you on a date." I paused and blew a smoke ring. "Nope. Sorry. No can do."

Jimmer shook his finger at me. "I had a damn date last night. I know how to treat a lady, unlike *some* guys."

Was that a shot at Martinez? And wasn't it ironic it was justified this time? Wasn't I chickenshit for not asking Jimmer if he knew whether Martinez was stepping out on me and why?

"Anyway, I'm here because I need a favor."

I'd say yes to anything to take my mind off cheaters and cheating and stupid Valentine's Day. "Sure. We waiting until Kev gets back?"

"Nope. This is just between you and me, little missy."

Anticipating a chance to kick some ass, I tucked a couple of zip-ties in my pocket. I decided to leave my gun, figuring Jimmer probably had an extra one on his person I could borrow and slipped on my black down parka. I practically skipped down the stairs with excitement.

Jimmer rarely drove the same car twice, so I did a double take at seeing his big body in the tiny blue Metro, idling by the curb. I hopped in and he cut across three lanes of traffic connecting two city blocks, the bald tires spinning on the ice. For a brief second I thought he was dragging me to Bare Assets to face Tony, but he parked in front of Victoria's Garden, the flower shop that sat down the block from the strip club. Then he bailed out of the car, leaving me no choice but to duck inside the shop after him.

Customers were in line at the register and I noticed other employees frantically arranging posies at work tables in the back. The humid scent of flowers and dirt clung in the air, reminding me of a cemetery.

I snagged Jimmer's coat sleeve. "Dude. You took a wrong turn. You realize we're in a flower shop, right?"

"You're fucking hilarious. Yes, I know where we are. I need to buy something for Valentine's Day for this... ah... woman I'm seeing." He shuffled his combat booted feet.

Jimmer, nervous? Really? After all the crap he'd given me over the years, now, I could totally razz him. "This was your big favor? I don't get to shoot stuff up or knock bad guys' dicks in the dirt? You need my help picking out... hearts and flowers and lovey-dovey shit?"

"Uh, yeah."

"Who is this for?"

"You don't know her. Which is why I need to cover all the bases, since I ain't even been to first base with her yet."

A smart remark dried on my tongue when I noticed the flush on his cheeks. My badass, gun-toting, pawnshop-owning friend was clearly flustered by his feelings for this woman.

So being a sucker for this big guy's sweet side, I took pity on him and dialed back my anti-Valentine's Day attitude. "I'll pick something flashy. And phallic." We browsed the buckets of fresh flowers lining the sales floor. We inspected shiny green plants. We studied exotic single blooms in fancy vases. Too many colors and styles caused an expression of pure panic on Jimmer's face.

That's when Lulu noticed us. I'd heard rumors that Lulu had traded in her pasties at Bare Assets for working with pansies at the flower shop. We knew each other in passing from hanging out at the Hombres clubhouse since she had an on again off again thing with Buzz, one of Martinez' bodyguards.

Lulu squealed when she saw Jimmer and squeezed him tight. "Big J! You naughty rascal I've missed seeing you."

Big J?

"And I've missed seeing you spinning on that pole, sugar plum."

Sugar plum?

Lulu glanced over her shoulder. "Now, don't you be telling secrets outta turn, Big J. I'm tryin' to be respectable." She patted his arm and cooed, "What can I help you with?"

"I need something for Valentine's Day."

I should've walked out right then; it was obvious Jimmer didn't need my help. But I stayed out of voyeuristic curiosity. Could lovely Lulu coax notoriously cheap Jimmer into forking over a big pile of bones so he could get to first base with his mysterious lady friend?

"You thinking flowers? Candy? A stuffed animal?"

"All of 'em. Probably."

Lulu playfully hip-checked Jimmer. "Sounds like someone else has fallen down the rabbit hole into love. Seems to be an epidemic with tough guys of late." Lulu winked at me. "Wouldn't you agree, Julie?"

I blinked. Then my gaze narrowed. Was she being sarcastic?

Jimmer scowled. "I ain't in love. If that's what she'll think if I send her flowers, then I'll just give her an AR-15 and a Snickers bar."

"No need to be hasty, I was just funning with ya, Big J," Lulu assured him. "The display case has lots of beautiful arrangements."

I tuned out their conversation, my sour thoughts flashing back to the first time my ex-husband had brought me flowers. On Valentine's Day. Trying to worm his way back into our bed after I'd confirmed the son of a bitch had cheated on me. Whenever his stories hadn't matched up, and whenever he'd showered me with flowers, I'd assumed he'd been dipping his wick elsewhere again. Did that make me just like Natalie Brunson's husband? Believing that once a cheater, always a cheater?

If Martinez was cheating on me, could I forgive him?

What if you've misread the situation?

If I really thought about it… seemed I always jumping to the wrong conclusions when it came to Tony Martinez.

Maybe I needed to take a big breath and stop thinking the worst.

"Hey Julie! How did you like the flowers?" Lulu asked, interrupting my thoughts.

"Those?" I pointed to the surprisingly tasteful bouquet Jimmer had selected. "They're great."

"Not these. I'm talking about the dozen-and-a-half white roses Mr. Martinez bought the day before yesterday."

My body went motionless. "What roses?"

"The ones he picked up when he was in here with Buzz. He bought us out of white ones."

I blinked at her.

"You sure it was Tony?" Jimmer asked.

What a stupid question. Of course Lulu knew it was Tony. She used to work for him.

An uncomfortable silence distorted the sickly-sweet air.

Lulu laughed a bit loudly. "Forget I said anything." She beamed at Jimmer. "Cash or credit?"

I said, "I'll wait outside."

Even the air seemed extra cold on my burning cheeks. I considered walking back to the office. Or straight to the closest bar, which ironically enough, my cheating bastard of a boyfriend owned.

I paced and smoked and examined the facts.

Fact 1: Tony had been physically and emotionally scarce in recent months.

Fact 2: He hadn't denied he was cheating when directly asked after I smelled perfume on him.

Fact 3: I saw him having coffee with a woman today and his bodyguard lied about it.

Fact 4: He'd purchased flowers I hadn't seen... two days ago.

Yeah, wasn't a big fucking leap to put two and two together and it added up to him indulging in foreplay with someone else.

I didn't know whether to scream or cry. Or ask Jimmer if I could borrow an AK47 for an hour or so.

Jimmer exited the flower shop with empty hands and he wore that pissed off look I recognized.

Probably pointless to deflect but I tried anyway. "Where are the pretty posies?"

"Bein' delivered along with the candy and balloons. Now tell me what the fuck is going on between you and Martinez."

"Why, whatever do you mean?" I batted my eyelashes. "Everything is rainbow-colored sprinkles and lollipops. And I hope for Lulu's sake she doesn't tell Buzz that she probably ruined Martinez' Valentine's Day surprise for me."

"You're lying."

I stood on tiptoe to poke him in the chest. "Yes, I am. But drop it."

"I'm gonna drop kick that motherfucker into next week—"

"Huh-uh, butt out. I'll handle it. Promise me you'll mind your own beeswax this time."

Jimmer looked torn. He loved to rip Martinez a new one when it came to his treatment of me. But I rarely asked him to promise me anything, so he knew I was dead serious.

"I'm agreeing to this under protest."

"So noted."

He didn't speak again until his piece of junk car idled in front of our building. "Keep me in the loop, Julie. Don't do nothin' stupid."

"Like what?"

"Like letting him get away with this."

The day deteriorated from there.

Loud voices echoed down the hallway. Marcia Bueller shouting at Glen Bueller. Kevin attempting to keep the peace while the redheaded home wrecker watched the scene unfold with a smug smile on her painted lips.

No one noticed my approach until I said, "Maybe we oughta take this into the conference room before someone calls the cops."

The trio marched into the office after Kevin.

I popped three aspirin before joining them. Everyone stood in a tight circle of anger.

"What is wrong with you?" Marcia demanded of her husband. "She's only two years older than our daughter!"

"Age is just a number, Marcia," Meghan inserted.

"It's Mrs. Bueller to you, you little conniving bitch. Show me proper respect."

"Marcia. Stop it." Glen sighed. "This isn't working."

"It was working fine until you quit your position in the firm and she went to work for you."

"You are in denial that anything was fine. Dammit, Marcia, can't you just admit we've both been miserable for years?'

"Years? My god. What is wrong with you? We haven't been miserable!"

"So that's why you hired a private detective? Because we're so blissfully happy?"

Marcia snapped back, "I hired him to find out if you were having an affair."

"Clearly, I am."

"And you don't have an ounce of remorse." Her eyes became small slits. "You wanted me to find out."

Glen nodded.

"So we could fix it?"

God, it was like a punch in the gut to hear the thread of hope in her voice.

"There's only one fix for this." Glen paused. "A divorce."

"No. You're having some kind of midlife crisis. We've been married thirty-five years, Glen. We'll go to counseling."

Glen shook his head. "Too late. I want a different life than you do."

"A life with her? Because she's willing to spread her legs for you anytime you ask?"

"Hey, that's not fair. It's more than sex between us."

No one paid attention to Meghan's half-assed protest.

Glen blurted, "You make me feel old, Marcia. And you have since I was a young man of thirty. I'm tired of planning for the future. Why can't I live in the now?"

"Because, despite acting like one, you're not a teenager," she sneered. "You're a professional man with commitments and responsibilities."

"And they've been a noose around my neck. And my balls. A noose I'm finally starting to loosen." He squared his narrow shoulders. "I intend to spend my remaining time living the life I should have. Regardless if that life is with Meghan."

That floored me. And Meghan apparently.

All the blood drained from Marcia's face. "Are you dying or something? Is that why you've made all these drastic changes in the last year?"

"If dying a little inside every day counts... then yes. I'm dying. The life we have together is slowly killing me."

Ooh. That was harsh.

The elegant Mrs. Bueller screeched like a barn owl. Her hand shot out so fast I didn't see it connect with Glen's face until the sharp crack echoed. The second slap included a swipe from her talons that left angry red welts on his skin from his cheek to the collar of his shirt.

We all stood there in stunned silence.

Then I saw Marcia twitch. I quickly stepped in front of her as she launched an attack at Meghan. Her wild swing caught me in the side of the head. Although tweety-birds spun in my vision, I managed to keep focused on my training and swept her feet out from beneath her. Then I flipped her on her stomach, pulled a zip tie out of my pocket and secured her arms behind her back. I resisted throwing my hands up in the air like a champion tie-down calf roper.

Glen and Meghan gaped at me, no surprise, but I *was* surprised by the flabbergasted look my partner leveled on me.

I bristled. "What?"

Kevin jammed a hand through his hair. "When did you learn to do that and... Why?"

"We're in the bond enforcement business now. I just proved how fast I can take down a threat." Probably over the top, but I cracked my knuckles. "Dog the bounty hunter ain't got nothin' on me, hoss."

"Here's a threat, you psychotic idiot. I will sue you if you don't unhand me right now," Marcia snapped.

Unhand me? Had I stumbled into a Shakespearian farce? I looked at Kevin.

"Thanks, Jules. Go ahead and finish your other report in your office, I'll take it from here."

Wasn't that a kick in the ass? Dismissed for taking my job performance to the next level. On behalf of all the ladies who'd come face-to-face with the other woman, I realized too late that I should've let Marcia pummel Meghan into the carpet. Hell. I should've held her.

I slammed my office door and smoked the afternoon away. Pacing, trying to figure out my next move. Did I confront Tony? Let it ride? Or did I hand him his walking papers?

Hour one: confronting him was the frontrunner.

Hour two: walking away from him took the lead.

By hour three… I wondered if I even owned a spine as I considered forgiveness.

Kevin entered my office. "Sorry about earlier with the Buellers. You just had that look in your eye and it never bodes well for anyone."

"What look?"

"Blood." He cocked a hip on my desk. "So, Smokey the grouchy bear, you've been more pissy than usual the last couple days. And your thug boyfriend hasn't stopped by. What's up with that?"

Kevin was not only my business partner, but my oldest friend. I was tired of sucking it up, mucking it up, putting on a tough girl front when it came to my relationship with Martinez. I needed to vent. I needed some advice. And it appeared Kev was offering. "How about if we trot down to the pub and I'll fill you in over a pint or ten?"

"Is that your way of asking me to be your Valentine?" he asked with a snicker.

"Fuck off."

Sanford's Pub and Grill has quirky junk tacked on the walls, like old license plates and metal advertising signs from the 40s and 50s. We headed to our usual table in the corner. Kevin ordered an Oil Can stout, a beer as dark and thick as Molasses. I ordered the Irish red.

Couples started pouring in. Happy duos out on a date for Valentine's Day. Smooching. Holding hands. Sharing a plate of half-price appetizers. I wondered how many of them were cheaters.

A hot, young scantily clad woman in ass-baring short shorts and a nipple-baring bra two sizes too small—sashayed up to our table, holding a tray of flowers. "Would you like to buy a rose for your lady?" she cooed to Kevin.

I slammed my beer mug down and growled, "I'm not anybody's goddamn lady."

She scampered off like a scolded pup.

Kevin sighed. "Scaring off the waitstaff? That's a new low even for you. Start talking."

My beer had gone warm by the time I'd finished my tale of woe.

Kev didn't say anything. He just continued to make water rings on the bar napkin with the bottom of his beer glass. When he finally looked up at me, I did not see the *Martinez is an asshole* solidarity I expected.

"What?"

"You're such a girl sometimes."

That got my back up. "Excuse me?"

"This 'whatever should I do' hand-wringing Julie in front of me? That's not you. The chick who threw a woman on her face today and zip-tied her hands? That's you. *That's* the Julie who should be dealing with this Martinez problem."

Odd thing? I didn't get all prickly and defensive because Kevin was right. I'd let a lot of stuff slide with Martinez. I'd been the dutiful girlfriend. Giving him space. Not interfering with his work. Waiting for him to come to me. Waiting for him to come clean.

No more.

Kevin laughed. "Now that's the look I was hoping to see."

"Which look is that?"

"You. Loaded for bear." He grinned. "Happy Valentine's Day, killer."

I bussed Kevin's cheek and slipped out the door.

~*~

Revved up by Kevin's advice, I drove to Fat Bob's.

The parking lot was jammed and a short line of people waited in the frigid air to get inside. Nothing said love on Valentine's Day like hanging out in a skanky biker bar.

I skirted the bouncer, who snagged the back of my coat. As Martinez' "old lady" I'd always just waltzed in. "Do you know who I am?"

"Yeah. A pain in my ass. ID. Cover charge."

"I don't ever pay a cover. Ask Cal. Ask Zee. Ask Big Mike."

He crossed his arms over his chest. "I don't know who you think you are—"

"I'm Martinez' girlfriend."

"Girlfriend?" he sneered. "So who is the chick in his office right now?"

I froze.

"That's what I thought. She's been comin' around for over a month. You haven't. You think I haven't heard the *I'm Martinez' girlfriend* line from all the ladies who show up here, wanting a piece of him?"

All the ladies? That jerk-off Martinez had a lot of explaining to do. "Fine. I'll pay the damn cover charge."

"Nope. Get lost. Don't make me get ugly with you."

"Too late on the ugly part since you were born that way. And you can't stop me from going in."

"Wanna bet?" When he lifted his lard ass off his stool, I rushed him. I whacked him in the head to divert attention from the kick I leveled at his knee. The kick knocked him off balance and his butt hit the dirt. I raced into the bar. Yeah, those self-defense lessons Jimmer gave me for Christmas were really working out great. I'd used them twice in one day.

Not quite wall-to-wall people inside, but close. I ducked, bobbed and weaved until I reached the door that led to the storage areas and Tony's office. I punched in the code and the door opened.

Let the fireworks begin.

Bodyguard and Hombres Enforcer Cal manned the door at the end of the corridor and stood as I stomped toward him. "Julie? What the hell are you doing here?"

"I want to see Martinez."

"Not a good idea."

I took two steps closer and Cal blocked me. "Move."

"I can't. You know that."

I ducked under his arm and pounded on the outer wall. "Martinez, you bastard, I know you're in here. Let me in right fucking now or I swear to god I will beat on this wall until it caves in." When that didn't work I started throwing punches, yelling obscenities, generally making a nuisance of myself that couldn't be ignored.

Feet shuffled rapidly on the concrete behind me and I spun around.

The angry weebil bouncer shambled toward me, with Corny, another of Martinez' two billion bodyguards, hot on his heels. When the bouncer lunged, Cal stepped in front of me.

"I suggest you take a step back, Paco."

"I want Mr. Martinez to know it wasn't my fault that she got in here unescorted. That bitch cold-cocked me!"

I returned to slamming my hands into the wall. "I mean it, Tony. Open the mother-fucking door."

Before I launched another attack on concrete, Corny inserted himself between me and the wall and gently pushed me back. "Julie, come on. This isn't helping. You know he'll be pissed off you're hurting yourself."

"Then I'm gonna put the hurt on him." Breathing hard, I stared at Corny's goofy smile, like my enraged state amused him.

"Who the fuck is she?" Paco demanded.

"Martinez' live-in girlfriend," Corny replied.

Paco's gaze raked over me. "If she's the girlfriend, then who is the brunette in there with him?"

"Exactly what I want to know." I sidestepped Corny and got in Cal's face. "Unlock the door and let me in."

His eyes held something akin to sympathy. Like he was trying to protect me from what I'd see behind that door.

Fuck that.

"Now. Or I'll pull out my gun and start firing at whatever the fuck strikes my fancy."

"Jesus, she's armed?" Paco shouted.

"Always," Corny replied with entirely too much cheer.

"Big Mike ain't gonna be happy," Cal said. He sighed and opened the door.

The fucking thing wasn't even locked. So it wasn't like Martinez was trying to hide the new chickie feathering his nest.

My fury escalated.

Big Mike rose from his spot inside the door.

Whoa. Had this place changed in the last month. A new concrete wall lined the entryway. I skirted Big Mike and made a beeline for the inner door.

But Big Mike caught me in one of those bodyguard bear hugs that are impossible to break free from. He managed to separate me from my purse and toss it to someone.

"Let me go!"

"What are you going to do if I do?"

"Since you took my gun and I can't shoot his dick off, I'm gonna kick his sorry lying ass."

Big Mike muttered, "'Bout damn time," and released me with a growled, "go get 'em, tiger."

I burst into the room.

Immediately, Martinez was on his feet, intercepting me. "Julie?"

But I didn't look at him. My eyes were firmly on the man-stealing bimbo perched on the edge of Tony's couch. I didn't stop moving until I loomed over her. "Is this the one whose perfume I smelled on you? The one you had coffee with? The one you gave the flowers to?"

"What the hell are you talking about?"

I whirled on Martinez. "Don't play stupid. Lulu told me you bought white roses two days ago. Did you give those to her?"

"Blondie. Take a deep breath."

"Like hell." I invaded the woman's space until I saw every pore on her face. "You want him? You'll have to go through me first to get him. So stand up."

She'd gone pale as a zombie.

"Get up right fucking now or I'll pull you up by your hair."

"Jesus, Julie, stop it," Martinez snapped.

His anger just fueled mine. "You willing to fight for him? Because I sure as fuck am." I closed my hands into fists, planning exactly where I'd place the first punch. "Get to your feet and show me what you've got."

"Please don't hurt me." She scooted away until her spine hit the back couch cushion. "Oh. My. God. Is that your blood? Or blood from the last person you beat up?"

I briefly glanced down at my knuckles, skinned up and bloodied from punching the wall.

"Why the hell is Julie bleeding?" Martinez demanded of Cal.

"I won't be the only one bleeding if someone doesn't tell me what the hell is going on."

The cornered woman began to babble. "Mr. Martinez hired my design firm to reconfigure the office spaces here and at Bare Assets."

"You can't lie worth shit. You're meeting with Tony in his private office, at a biker bar, to discuss a work project... on Valentine's Day? Not buying it."

"But it's true! There can't be any record of the redesign plans because of his security issues, so he hired me off the books to do this and some, ah, other stuff. The only time we can meet is after hours."

"Then why did you have coffee with him in public at Dunn Brothers this morning?"

No response. Tony didn't jump in to explain either.

I fumed. The fact this interloper wore skintight jeans, a fringed leather halter and stiletto boots pegged my bullshit meter. "Don't you Martha Stewart types usually go for a classier style than slutty biker bitch?"

I heard Big Mike laugh and cover it with a cough before Martinez snarled at him.

She started to get off the couch. "I really need to go now."

"Stay. Put. You move and I'll tackle your bony butt to the ground before I kick it."

"That's enough," Martinez barked. "Julie. Back off. Now."

"Kiss my ass, Martinez. This is between me and her. Get a bucket because I'm gonna wipe the floor with her."

"For Christ's sake... Mike. Grab her."

Before I could land a single punch, steel bands crushed my arms to my sides. I thrashed while Little Miss Interior Design scurried out like the rat she was.

Once she was out of my sight, Big Mike carried me to the bedroom, tossed me on the bed and locked me in.

What the hell was that about?

I leapt off the bed in such a state of fury I tripped and fell on my hands and knees. First thing I noticed was the stanky-ass army green shag had been replaced with plush dark brown carpet. I looked around the room, scarcely recognizing the space. It resembled a pricey hotel suite, with a king-sized bed, a small sitting area, built in bookcases surrounding a big screen TV. I pushed to my feet and opened the door to what used to be a closet. Holy crap. Talk about a fancy bathroom. Done up in black and white with chrome fixtures, with a glass-walled shower, two pedestal sinks and one entire wall covered in mirrored tiles.

The space smelled like Tony so I knew this was where he'd been staying. Had he fixed this up because he needed a place to get away... from me?

That hurt worse than the idea he was cheating on me.

A wave of nausea scalded my insides, followed by a white-hot slice of pain. If there'd been a window, I would've crawled out of it.

Stumbling back to the bedroom, I perched on the edge of the bed, waiting to be released from my private hell, caught in this gilded cage that hadn't been built for me.

When the locks clicked, I fought my natural urge to come up swinging.

"Julie?" Big Mike said gently. "Tony is waiting for you."

"I don't give a..." I bit the inside of my cheek until I tasted blood. I would not give him the satisfaction of my anger. I sure as hell wouldn't cry. Fuck him. I wouldn't even obey his edict.

Holding my head up, I left the posh bedroom and kept walking right on by the living area where Tony waited.

"Where the hell do you think you're going?" Martinez asked.

"As far away from you as I can get." In the entryway, I looked on the floor for my purse.

No sign of it.

Cal blocked the only exit. If Tony told him to keep me in, I was trapped. Even if I did manage to make it out, I had no keys. No cell phone. No money.

Bastards. Every fucking one of them.

I pressed my back against the wall, slid to the floor and rested my forehead on my knees, curling into a tight ball. Martinez had no right to make me feel this way. Like I'd stepped over the line. This was his fault. Not mine. I had to force myself to breathe slowly and steadily or I'd turn into a raging lunatic. Or maybe I already was.

Voices bounced to me. Big Mike's. Tony's. Corny's. Not hers. Had Tony sent her away from his psycho soon to be ex-girlfriend?

A knee popped and leather creaked as someone knelt in front of me. My heart raced.

"Blondie."

"Leave me alone, Martinez."

"No."

His callused fingertips touched my face and I flinched.

But that didn't deter him. He kept stroking my cheek. "Look at me."

Petulant girl wanted to deny his command. I managed to meet his gaze, but jerked my head from his touch.

Tony had gone beyond pissed off to the lethally quiet anger that made everyone around him tread lightly.

Of course, I didn't pay any heed. "Give me back my damn purse."

"I shouldn't ever give it back since you showed up here armed."

I raised my chin and stared at him coolly. "Keep the stupid gun. You gave it to me anyway. Just let me go."

"Fine. Corny will get your truck and drive you home. He's on duty at ten tonight." He rose, said something, and Corny took off.

Without asking permission, I walked to the back door and bailed outside. When my pickup pulled up, I motioned Corny to the passenger side so I could drive. My purse was in the seat. I fired up a Marlboro so fast I nearly singed my fingertips.

For once I was glad my Hombres babysitter was silent. I smoked one cigarette after another, obsessing that Martinez had neither confirmed nor denied sexual involvement with the slutty Martha Stewart wannabe.

Did he really think I'd sweep this under the rug?

No. He knew me better than that. *I* knew me better than that. I'd set the fucking rug on fire. Then I'd beat it down with the broom until nothing remained but cinders in my search for the truth.

After parking in the garage, I entered my side of the house, slamming the door in Corny's face. In my foul mood, I saw two choices. Blurring the edges of my anger with Don Julio tequila, or taking my frustrations out on Martinez' punching bag.

Why not do both?

I snatched the tequila, changed into baggy boxing shorts and a black sports bra before I headed upstairs. Tony was a fiend about working out and had installed a full gym in the extra bedroom. I took a long pull off the bottle before I slipped on a pair of weight lifting gloves. I cranked the Drowning Pool tracks on the iPod stereo and started warming up with the heavy bag.

Not hard at first. Just a steady connection of my fists to canvas. My muscles loosened. My resolve strengthened.

First, I saw Natalie Brunson's face. One slip-up and destined to be branded a cheater forever.

Right. Left. Right. Right. Right.

Then I saw Glen Bueller's face. Too much of a wuss to verbally confront his wife about their marriage issues.

Right. Left. Right. Left.

Then I saw my cheating ex-husband's face when I'd caught him, yet again, with lipstick on his collar and his zipper undone.

Fucker. I swigged from the bottle and went back to beating on the bag as "Bodies" blasted from the speakers.

Jab. Jab. Jab. Right uppercut. Left uppercut. Jab. Jab. Jab. Left uppercut. Right uppercut.

Martinez' face swam into view and I blinked the sweat from my eyes.

Sweat, goddammit. Not tears. I hit the bag harder. And harder. Pissed off at him. Pissed off at myself. Scared I was so in love with him I'd forgive him anything. Even infidelity.

I pummeled the bag until I couldn't stay upright. Until I had to sag against the canvas to catch my breath. But I could still reach the tequila and I sucked down two long swallows.

"You're hesitating during that sequence," Martinez said behind me. "Your body language gives away your intent."

"Everyone's a critic." I peeled off the gloves and used a towel to mop my face. I sensed his hard stare as I booked it from the room.

I'd reached the kitchen when a strong hand on my bicep spun me around.

"Jesus, Julie, you're bleeding." Before I uttered a word, Tony herded me to the sink and shoved my hands under cold water. Then he stomped to the adjoining door and threw it open. "Mike, get in here and bring your first aid kit."

Rather than stir the pot further, I kept my mouth firmly closed. I didn't fight when Martinez gently dried my hands and settled me in a kitchen chair. Big Mike applied antibacterial ointment and bandages to my ravaged knuckles. When Tony paced in front of me, I sure as hell didn't ask why he'd changed into workout attire similar to mine, long black boxing shorts and a skin-tight wife beater. How cute. We even wore matching sneers.

As soon as Big Mike finished, he disappeared through the adjoining door. A door that Martinez locked.

A door that was never locked from our side.

Oh, this was not a good sign.

I had the overwhelming urge to run.

Then I heard the sliding glass door open and close behind me. I didn't turn around.

"You calmed down?" he asked.

"Don't try to placate me, Martinez. I have a right to be pissed."

"Do you?"

"Yes." I looked at my bandaged knuckles.

Martinez moved in front of me and tossed something at my feet. "Lulu was right. I bought flowers. For you. Wanna see them? Go ahead," he said. "They're pretty, aren't they? Pretty fucking dead."

I saw a blackish-green stems sticking out from the end of dull green wax paper. If I used my imagination I could see that the brown, crinkled heads had been white blooms at one time. I'd never been so happy to see dead flowers in my life. I finally glanced at him.

Tony was in his usual defiant posture. Arms crossed. Jaw rigid. His face, his beautiful, masculine face, held a look I'd never seen.

"What happened?"

"Evidently, I wasn't supposed to leave them on the seat of my car for eighteen hours when it's below zero." He threw up his hands. "How was I supposed to know that? I've never bought goddamn flowers for a woman in my life. And when I do? I kill them and then you think I've been..."

Cheating. Showering another woman with flowers that should've been mine.

Some of the doubts plaguing me lessened. Some, not all. I picked up the bouquet. Frozen solid.

"I didn't notice they looked like that until it was too late. I was too... fucking embarrassed to show you that night. Christ. I couldn't even laugh about it. So I hid them on the deck."

You sweet, stupid, prideful man.

Of course, I couldn't say that. But I probably shouldn't have said, "Tony, are you cheating on me?" either.

A heartbeat or two passed.

"That's the second time you've asked me that."

"And that's the second time you haven't answered a direct question from me."

He sighed.

I'd had it. I got up and walked out.

Halfway up the stairs I heard him say, "Where are you going?"

"To get my snow boots because it's getting deep in here."

I figured he'd follow me. I returned to the workout room for my tequila. I'd taken a couple of healthy sips and looky there. Mr. Bad Boy himself lounged in the doorway, every muscled, tattooed inch a feast for my senses.

"You shouldn't be drinking while you're working out," he said.

"You shouldn't be in here giving me shitty advice when I'm pissed off at you and drinking," I retorted.

Martinez smiled. "I'll take my chances." Then he stalked me.

I didn't offer him any Don Julio before I set it on the floor. We faced each other on the sparring mat. Circling, crouching, about to change the parameters of this fight.

"You wanna go a couple rounds with me?" Martinez asked. "Shadow boxing? No contact?"

I snorted. "Dude. Weren't you like Colorado's Golden Gloves Boxing champion or something?"

"National Champion in my weight class. Three years running." He did some fancy footwork, a fast-jabbing set of moves that showcased his skill, his power and highlighted his lean, muscular physique. "It's what paid my way through college."

This is what I missed. Us together, talking, hanging out, discovering new little things about each other, like any other normal couple. But Martinez was a master at distracting me. And I'd started to fall for it again without getting the answers I deserved.

I planned to tackle him, using my new self-defense skills—third time was a charm—but before I made my move the sneaky fucker was all up in my face.

"So that's a *no* to shadow boxing? Fine. Then we'll grapple."

I'd barely opened my mouth to protest, when I found myself spun around, flipped flat on my back on the mat and Tony hanging on all fours above me.

I laid there like a log.

"Come on, blondie. Fight back."

"I'm tired of fighting with you, Martinez."

His eyes searched my face. "You sure?"

"Yes."

"Good." He lowered his mouth to mine. His kiss wasn't passionate. Wasn't sweet. It was thorough. Very, very thorough in the way that heated my blood, fuzzed my brain and damn near liquefied my bones.

He pulled back from the kiss with great reluctance. His gaze bored into mine. "Julie."

"Tony."

We stared at each other, breathing hard, eyes guarded.

"Last chance," I said softly. "Tell me the truth. Either way. I have to know."

"You really gonna make me say it to you?"

I nodded, hating how fast my heart beat in those four seconds before his mouth moved.

"I am not cheating on you. I'd *never* cheat on you."

I waited, watching his facial expression change from wariness to fierceness.

"I love you. I love you like a fuckin' mad man. How can you not know that? How could you believe, even for a split second, that I'd ever look at another woman, touch another woman, when I have you in my life and in my bed?" He twined a section of my long hair around his finger and pulled hard enough to get my attention. "Jesus, blondie. What will it take to convince you that I'm not fucking around when we've got this between us? You're it for me. You always will be."

In that moment, I felt the truth of his words lodge deep within me, in a place where doubt couldn't get a foothold. This life-hardened man, who never showed anyone weakness, reminded me that I was his safe haven. I gave him something he couldn't get from anyone else. He did the same for me. I reached up and curled my hand around his face. "I miss you."

"Same." Tony kissed the crook of my elbow. "I gotta admit as shitty as these last two months have been, I seriously got off on you storming into my office today and showing that tough-girl side I haven't seen in a while."

"You did?"

Martinez flashed the devilish grin that usually made me start stripping. "Yeah. Would you really have fought for me?"

"In a heartbeat. First, I would've kicked her ass. Then yours." I pulled him down for another kiss. A hotter kiss. The kind of deep soul kiss that brought forth his primitive growl. I trailed my lips up the strong line of his jaw, to his ear. "I love you. The thought of you leaving me for someone else..."

"Blondie," he murmured in my hair, "that ain't ever gonna happen."

He eased back when I sat up.

"You say that... but I'm just supposed to ignore the signs of you pulling away? You prefer sleeping at Fat Bob's or Bare Assets to sleeping with me. We moved in together to be together. And then I find out you've been turning your private office spaces into personal living spaces? Like you needed a place to get away from me."

"That's what you think?"

"I don't know what to think."

"I think your nosiness, Miz PI"—he lightly touched the tip of my nose—"has ruined my big surprise for you."

"Yeah, right. So explain the bimbo in your office. And why you had coffee with her today."

He sighed at my skeptical look and grabbed the tequila, taking a swig. "You don't give an inch, do you?"

I shrugged and snatched the bottle from him.

"I hired Gina, the interior design specialist that you so charmingly threatened tonight, to upgrade office interiors while we shored up external security issues. As we were talking, I mentioned hating the place that you and I moved into, and I hated being bound to those same security precautions outside of the clubs."

"Still confused about why you couldn't tell me any of this."

Martinez rested on his haunches. "Guilt. You've given up a lot to be with me. And right before Thanksgiving, I realized I haven't met you halfway on anything."

"You sort of are the 'my way or the highway' guy, El Presidente."

"True. It's not fair to you. Not fair to tell you that your friends aren't allowed at our place. Anyway, Gina's been a go-getter since the Hombres, ah, *handled* her brother's problem last fall. She made the spaces at both Bare Assets and Fat Bob's less of an embarrassment for someone in my position. I thought maybe you'd be willing to crash there with me on nights I can't get home."

"I'd live in a milk crate with you," I murmured. "It's never been about atmosphere for us."

"I know, but you deserve a nice place. Anyway, Gina found two houses, side by side, in town, not way the fuck out in the middle of cow county like this place. Houses I purchased that are being retro-fitted to my security specs."

"Meaning bulletproof glass on the windows, steel doors, state-of-the-art security system," I said jokingly… and yet not.

"And an underground tunnel that links them." He flashed that wicked bad boy grin again. "A secret concrete room that could have some pretty interesting uses."

"Maybe Kevin was right about the biker kink and me investing in fetish wear."

His eyes lit up. "Would you really wear leather, latex and chains for me?"

"Hah! Nice try, pervert."

"But you didn't say *no*," he pointed out with another panty-melting grin.

"Back to the issue… why the secrecy?"

"It's something we haven't tried since I took over as president of the Hombres and we didn't want word getting out ahead of time that my security team will live in one house. We'll live in the other. By ourselves."

That was a huge concession for him. "Seriously?"

"Yes." Martinez trapped my face in his hands. "The reason I haven't been coming home? This place is too far to drive when I'm tired and I don't get done with business until three o'clock in the morning. This move in together was supposed to fix that. It hasn't."

"When did you plan on telling me about the new house?"

His thumbs stroked the hollow of my cheeks.

Then I knew. "Shit. Please tell me you weren't planning it as a Valentine's Day surprise?"

"Give me a little credit. I know how much you hate Valentine's Day. That's why I bought the damn flowers two days *before* Valentine's Day. The contractor told me the changes would be done by next week. Then you could start picking all the inside stuff."

"You're letting me pick? You're not having Little Miss Interior Designer choose like she's done with everything else?" Wow. That'd come out a little snarky.

"Big Mike called that one," he muttered.

"What's that mean?"

"Big Mike said you'd be pissed that I was keeping you in the dark about everything. From the interior changes in the offices, to buying a new place without your input, to hiring Gina. He also said he couldn't wait to see you blow your top because it's always so damn entertaining." Martinez shook his head. "I get that I should've told you, okay? The only reason we met Gina in public today was because her car died right at Dunn Brothers and I needed a damn cup of coffee."

"Riding in your Escalade to rescue the damsel in distress?"

He looked annoyed for about five seconds and then he smiled. "Makes me a Neanderthal, but I love seeing that jealous spark, blondie."

I rolled my eyes.

"Besides. I prefer damsels who don't need rescuing. Like you."

"Such sweet bullshit. But I'll take it."

"And?" he prompted.

"And I'm sorry I didn't jump your shit before tonight."

He gave me that exasperated noise that was half snort/half sigh.

That's when I knew we'd be okay. I grabbed the bottle of tequila, but Tony snatched it first. Keeping his eyes on mine, he lifted the bottle and drank. When I held my hand out for my turn, he shook his head. "Let me."

He pressed the opening to my lips and tipped the bottle. The amount of liquid he poured in was more than a quick sip and some spilled out the corner of my mouth. It started to drip down my neck and I reached up to swipe it away, but Tony stayed my hand. He grabbed a fistful of my hair and tilted my head back. His hot breath teased the wet section of my skin as he lowered his mouth and his tongue slowly followed the tequila trail up the side of my neck to my lips.

My entire body vibrated with want.

"That's the way to drink tequila. Warmed by your body with your skin as my salt lick." He nibbled my mouth, those dark hungry eyes burned into mine. "Clothes off."

Didn't have to tell me twice.

Didn't have to tell him either.

Naked, we stood and faced each other.

Tony reached out and trailed one finger from my lips, down my throat, between my breasts, stopping at my navel.

I shivered from his touch. I started to step forward, step into him, and he shook his head.

This round wouldn't be hard and fast. He took great care with every caress. Rough hands and a soft mouth eking out my sighs and moans. Then we were rolling around on the exercise mat and Martinez ended up on top.

I didn't mind.

He tasted each millimeter of my flesh from my chin to my toes and wouldn't change the languorous pace even if I begged. Which I did. Shamelessly. The man just chuckled against my quivering lower belly as his hot, wet kisses dropped lower and he settled between my thighs.

I sifted my hands through his silky hair as he slowly pushed me up that sharp rise and left me teetering on the brink until his relentless, clever mouth sent me tumbling into that vortex of pleasure.

Then Martinez exuded panther-like grace as he crawled back up my body.

The reverent touches vanished. Before I could catch my breath or wallow in the scent of his skin, he was on me, in me, and I lost coherent thought. Lost in the power of his passion. Lost in what we were together. Complete.

Afterward, as I lay face down on the mat, dizzy and sex-drunk, his gentle hands moved the hair from my damp face. He murmured, "So, am I forgiven?"

"Uh. Yeah."

"Good." He nuzzled my ear and I felt his body readying for another bout. The man had maintained that boxer's stamina over the years. He could go four rounds in one night.

Lucky me.

~*~

BAITED

A Julie Collins novella

Chapter 1~ Setting the Bait

My father never took me fishing as a child. Neither did he teach me to throw a ball or ride a bike. He occasionally showed me his backhand, though. So any resentment I have about missing those rites of adolescence remained trapped on the tip of my bloodied tongue.

Fishing expertise would have come in handy that morning. A guy I dubbed "Matchstick" strolled into the offices of Wells and Collins Investigations just as I was indulging in my third smoke break in thirty minutes. I'd had nothing to look forward to that day besides filing, and filing made me cranky.

"Can I help you?" I asked, eyeing the snappy slogan on his T-shirt—*It's not the size of the rod or how deep you fish, it's all in the way you wiggle the worm.*

"Uh, yeah." He frowned at the mess distinguishing my office from the reception area; folders heaped on the desk, fashion magazines strewn on the floor, the anodized ashtray overflowing with crimson tipped cigarette butts. "I'm looking for Kevin Wells."

"Sorry. Kevin is on assignment today. But I'd be happy to help you."

The man's questioning glance zoomed past my insubstantial breasts, traveled over the pinkish scars marring my throat and lingered on my mouth. Most men are spellbound by full lips like mine—they look as if they'd lost a round with a killer bee.

He blinked away whatever oral fantasy he'd fallen into and managed, "You his secretary then?"

"He wishes. I'm his partner, Julie Collins. And you are?"

"Rich Barber." He thrust a freckled, skeletal hand across my desk, which I took without pause, my manners intact. "Jimmer sent me. Said Kevin might be able to help me out. But if he's not available..."

"And Jimmer forgot to mention little ol' me?" I tsk-tsked. "Gender bias. That boy is in so much trouble next time I see him."

"Whoa." He backed up. "The last thing I need is a pissed off Jimmer Cheadle hot on my tail."

"Relax. I was kidding." My estimation of Mr. Barber jumped a notch if he was leery of my six-foot-six, ex-commando pal, Jimmer. "Have a seat." I pointed to the chair opposite my desk. "Tell me how you think I can help you."

Rich was wound so tight he bounced when his bony butt connected with the buffalo skin cushion. Without preamble he said, "My friend, JC, is missing and I think his wife killed him."

I let that sink in for a minute. I slowly ground out my cigarette. "Don't know what Jimmer told you, or what detective novels you read, but we don't investigate homicides. Contact Detective Mitch Jones at the Rapid City PD. In fact, I'll call him right now." I reached for the phone.

But Rich's cool, strong hand covered mine. "They know he's missing. His wife is the one who filed the report." His single red unibrow wrinkled above his flat nose. "Don't you read the paper? They did an article on his disappearance a couple of weeks ago."

I prefer to get my news from TV. Actually, I haven't read a newspaper since Ann Landers kicked the bucket and they'd discontinued her column. I've always taken perverse pleasure in knowing there are people out there with lives more screwed up than mine. "I must have missed that. If the police know he's MIA, why aren't you talking to them?"

His face turned the mottled reddish orange of a prairie sunset. "I tried. They umm...laughed."

That struck me as odd. Cops never discount any theory on a case, no matter how outrageous. "They laughed? Why?"

He squirmed. "Because I told them that JC's psycho wife, Cindy Jo

Cracken, probably wrapped an anchor around his neck and took him fishing."

I could imagine my friend Jimmer right now, standing in the hallway, holding his stomach in silent mirth, waiting to see how his latest practical joke had panned out. Last week he sent me an eighty-year old woman who demanded I find her lost libido. The thought of powdered wrinkles covered in sweat slapping against another body of sagging skin...Yuck. I couldn't have sex for two days.

Rich sighed. "Go ahead and laugh."

"So this *is* some kind of joke?"

He shook his head.

"Then you'd better start at the beginning." I unearthed a legal pad and waited, Bic pen poised, picture of PI efficiency.

"Four weeks ago my friend, JC Bettleyoun, disappeared. His wife claims he got in his truck and drove to Kansas City. No one has heard from him since."

"Why was he going to Kansas City?"

"Supposedly he was attending the regional American Bass Anglers Association meeting and he had an appointment with a potential sponsor."

"Bass?" I repeated inanely. "As in fish?"

"Yeah. JC was gonna try his luck as a professional bass fisherman."

Now I *knew* Jimmer had to be busting a gut someplace close. "Look—"

"You don't believe me either." Rich jumped up off the chair. "Never mind."

"Rich, sit down." He flopped back into the chair, his breath coming as fast and shallow as an air-starved goldfish. "I'm just surprised, is all. People *really* get paid to fish?"

The peculiar look on his face read; clueless female. "There's huge money in professional fishing. JC entered a couple of bass tournaments down south a year ago last summer when he and Cindy Jo were on vacation. Shocked the hell out of everyone when he actually won a few." He leaned forward over his spindly thighs, confiding, "See, JC is a pretty big talker, but he *never* follows through with anything. Know the kind of guy I mean?"

I nodded. That pretty much described most of the men I'd dated. With one exception. "Does he have a job?"

"The most successful thing JC ever did was marry Cindy Jo. Once they hooked up, he's never had to hold a regular job. He knows she'll haul out the checkbook whenever he runs short."

A sugar momma. How novel. "Was he proud of that?"

"At times." His cheeks bloomed when he realized he'd been trash-talking his buddy, but he pressed on. "I thought bein' at her beck and call was a high price to pay for the limited funds she doled out. Anyway, she made fun of him when he told her his plans to go pro. Said fishing was a hobby, not a job. That might've been the end of it, but JC has a mean streak a mile wide and the temper to match. So, during the sports show, this winter, he bought a brand new fishing boat."

Hardly grounds for murder, but I kept listening. "What did Cindy Jo do?"

"Hit the roof. Told him he'd better take it back to the dealership 'cause she wasn't paying for it."

"Where does Cindy Jo get her money?"

"She owns that nail salon off of Jackson—Hot Tips. Pretty successful place, I guess. She bought thirty acres outside of Hermosa and put a brand new double wide on it just last year."

"They have any children?"

"Not the normal kind." I lifted a brow and he rushed to explain, "Cindy Jo's twenty years older than JC. Never could have kids, but she does have them yippy damn dogs she calls her babies. Drove JC nuts, the way she pampered and fussed at them." His thin lips made a girlish moue of distaste. "When one vanished a few months back, I thought he'd have to admit her to the psych ward, the way she carried on."

"Still, the fact he bought a new fishing boat wasn't exactly reason to kill him." I relied on the old standby in our business: marital infidelity. "Was JC screwing around?"

Rich opened his mouth as if to laugh, but thought better of it. "No. JC was a jerk, and smart women avoided him. Truth is, he could've screwed any chick and Cindy Jo wouldn't have cared."

My skepticism must've showed.

"Sounds strange, but she was jealous of the time he spent fishing. She whined he paid more attention to his rods and reels than he did to her."

"And did he?"

"Well, yeah, especially after he bought the boat." A gusty sigh, like one might expect after a satisfying bout of sweaty sex, filled the room. "It is a sweet machine, with top of the line digital fish finder—"

"Which is all interesting," I interrupted his almost orgasmic reverie, "but where's Cindy Jo's motive?"

Rich scratched the red stubble on his chin. "That's what made Cindy Jo crazy. He didn't use *her* money to buy it. I don't know where JC scrounged up that kind of cash, but I have my suspicions. He figured since he'd paid for the boat, he didn't have to answer to Cindy Jo 'bout how much time he spent fishing. And, JC wouldn't even let her set foot on it."

"How'd that go over?"

"Guess she was mad enough to spit nails." He chortled at his own humor.

I bit back a smile. "So he up and went to Kansas City to prove he could be a pro fisherman without her blessing? Did you know he'd hooked a potential sponsor?"

"I don't know. I didn't even know he had a sponsor. He would've shared the news with me, or asked me to ride along, but I knew nothing about it. I heard it all from Cindy Jo."

Something didn't fit. "Would JC have asked you to come with him if he'd been doing something illegal on his way to Kansas City?"

Rich blanched but didn't answer, which in itself was the answer I needed.

"Could he be 'running errands'?" 'Running errands' is slang for drug trafficking on I-90—the interstate that bisects South Dakota. I had it on good authority that the highway patrol zeros in on out-of-state license plates, leaving local drug runners somewhat safe. Especially when the locals are willing to rat out a competitor from another state. The SDHP gets a big drug bust and the locals get to carry on, business as usual. "JC was into something bad, wasn't he?"

His morose nod made me feel as if I'd kicked a puppy, but I soldiered on. "Think about this. If he was running drugs, and if he double-crossed his new employers, his body may be moldering in the middle of a cornfield. And if that's the case, I doubt anyone will find him until threshing time."

His congenial tone disappeared and his eyes snapped with resentment. "That's a possibility, but Cindy Jo is involved somehow, I just know it. She killed him. Even if she is a little bitty thing, she's as mean as rattlesnake."

That stopped me for a second, but his line of logic lacked a hook. I hate turning down business, but I felt compelled to point out, "Still don't see the motive. She couldn't have killed him for a life insurance policy, because you have to produce a body to make the claim."

Rich picked at a hole in his ratty jeans, avoiding my gaze. Finally he glanced up at me with haunted, watery eyes. "Maybe I'm off base, but will you at least talk to Cindy Jo, even if it proves I'm the one that's crazy?"

Poor man. I didn't want to get his hopes up, but this whole situation smacked of a bad episode of *Maury Povich.* Luckily for him, I'd been born a sucker for a sad story with a rotten ending. "Sure. I'll talk to her, see what else I can find out," I said, withdrawing a blank contract from my desk, "but it'll cost you."

Red splotches appeared on his forehead, nearly matching the color of his hair. "How much?"

I immediately knocked off two hundred dollars from the standard retainer. "Three hundred to start. That'll buy you a day or so of seeing what I can dig up. Beyond that, I'll call you before you rack up any more charges. Will that work?"

He nodded.

I filled in the contract and handed him a pen. He nearly knocked off one of the glass statues on my desk as he maneuvered his arm around to sign the paperwork with his left hand.

After he'd signed on the dotted line, he stood, dug in the left front pocket of his skin-tight Wranglers, and tossed three crumpled sweaty Benjamins on top of the paperwork.

"One last question. Did JC take his boat with him to Kansas?"

"No. That's why I think he's dead. JC wouldn't take off and leave his boat behind. It meant more to him than anything and Cindy Jo knows that."

"So where is the boat again?"

"Still docked down at Angostura, far as I know. Slip twenty-seven, cherry red boat with a matching tarp. Thinking about checking it out?"

I shrugged. "Can't hurt."

"Do you know how to drive a boat?" His skepticism wasn't winning him any points.

I did have some boating experience, thanks to an ex-boyfriend who'd introduced me to the joys of water-skiing among other, less wholesome, but far more appealing water sports. "Why?"

"Cause my boat is docked down there. Not as fancy as JC's, but it runs." From a large key ring attached to his belt-loop, he extracted a black lanyard with two small keys and handed it over. "Take this in case you need an excuse about why you're poking around. The old guy that runs the bait shop is awful nosy."

"Thanks. How will I know which boat is yours?"

"Mine's the only one with a lighted bow fishing platform."

At my dubious look, Rich's crooked grin split from one big ear to the other.

"I'm an eighth Lakota. Bow hunting and bow fishing are the only parts of my heritage I actively pursue."

I considered his flaming red hair, blue eyes, toothpick body and lily-white skin. "An eighth Sioux, huh?"

"Got that same look when my *unci* dragged me to Pine Ridge and enrolled me in the tribe."

My Lakota language skills were pathetic but I recognized the word *oon-chi.* "Your grandmother?"

"Yep. Truth is, blood doesn't lie."

As I well knew. "My brother was from White Plain."

"Were you born there, too?" he asked, taking the high road, choosing not to judge me by my blond hair, blue eyes, high cheekbones and fair complexion.

I shook my head. "But I do some bow-hunting."

Pleasure warred with shock on his face. Pleasure won out. "What's your draw weight?"

"Fifty pounds. I just got a new composite bow." I left out the tiny detail that my previous bow had been forcibly retired after being used to kill a man. I'd found out the hard way that factoid did not always instill confidence in new clients.

We spent the next few minutes discussing the minutiae about bows that only enthusiasts would understand. After giving me a brief rundown on the basics of bow fishing, and how his particular equipment worked, he encouraged me to try it out. And I admit he'd hooked my interest. Maybe more so in trying my hand at bow fishing than in investigating this case.

"I gotta get to work; hate to blow my shot at 'Employee of the Month'." Rich winked. It wasn't an accomplished wink, or a lewd wink, but a shy wink from a man I imagined hadn't had much practice in the art of flirting.

Something unexpectedly sweet moved through me.

He turned to go, but stopped just inside the doorframe. "Say, if you happen to come across a knife on JC's boat, would you let me know? He borrowed it a couple of months back..." His ears turned pink. "It was a gift from my *unci*. She spent a lot of money on it after the sales guy convinced her it'd been specially made for lefties."

"But it wasn't?"

Rich shook his head. "No. It's not a switchblade. Most of them have a thumb release button on both sides, so they work for right and lefthanders. Mine is a fixed blade."

I blinked. I was learning all sorts of new stuff today. But all knives looked alike to me. "How will I know it's yours?"

"It's got a six inch blade with the brand name Boker etched in the steel. My initials RAB are carved on the bottom of the handle. If you find it, make sure it stays in the leather sheath. It's sharp."

"Thanks for the warning. I'll be in touch after I do some poking around."

His keys jangled against his bony hip as he left. I leaned back and lit another cigarette, deciding on my next move. Filing could wait; I had my first solo bona-fide case this week.

As I sat smoking, reflecting on everything I'd just heard I looked down at my ragged cuticles and bitten-to-the-quick nails. Since business was slow, this seemed like an ideal day to get a manicure.

~*~

Hot Tips was located in one of those 1980s low-slung shopping plazas. It was nestled between a travel agency and a chiropractor's office. The sign, once painted a trendy mauve, had faded into the grayish pink of a dead jellyfish. A brass bell tinkled as I pushed open the glass door.

The heavy scent of acetone greeted me, as well as the sounds of classic rock. High and low murmured tones of unrecognizable female conversation added to the background noise. I leaned on a kidney-shaped reception desk and expected to wait. I'd barely begun drumming my fingers on the desk when a peroxide blonde bounded from behind the burgundy privacy screen separating the waiting area from the main shop.

"Can I help you?"

"I'm here to see Cindy Jo."

She snatched up my right hand and scrutinized it. "I'll say. Sweet Lord in heaven look at this mess! And here I thought they'd outlawed pickin' cotton the same time as slavery. Girl," she drawled in her thick southern accent, "what have you been *doin'* to these poor things?"

Embarrassed, I tried to pull my unsightly hands away but it was impossible to fight against Miss Texarkana's firm grip. "I've never much been into the whole nail routine, so I thought I'd give it a shot."

"Then you've come to the right place, sugar, and from the looks of it not a minute too soon." Over her shoulder she yelled, "Cindy Jo? Your three o'clock is here."

I didn't bother to correct her.

Just then, the tiny woman I assumed was Cindy Jo strolled into view.

She had wide brown eyes framed by false eyelashes; deep-set wrinkles reached into her hairline. Against her tanned face, her black hair shone as bright as her capped teeth.

"One of these days, Mandy, you'll actually use that intercom instead of your lungs."

Mandy snorted indelicately.

Cindy Jo's gaze flicked over me before she zeroed in on my hands. Mandy checked out the backs, sweeping her thumb across my knuckles and the callused tips of my fingers.

"Good Lord," Mandy gasped when she flipped my hands over. "How did you get all those scars?" Gently, she traced a lavender nail over the puckered skin crisscrossing my palms. Her eyes locked with Cindy Jo's. "Maybe you oughta show her how the hot wax treatment is helping you, since your hands look just like this."

"Hush," Cindy Jo snapped, hiding her hands from view. "Get back to your station."

Once Mandy sauntered away, Cindy Jo smiled tightly. "Sorry. She's got more heart than brains. Hope she didn't offend you."

"Takes more than that to offend me."

"Good. Let's get started." She motioned for me to follow her. We didn't settle into one of the mirrored nail stations, but passed through a doorway in the back and entered a small paneled office with a tanning bed shoved in the corner. Cindy Jo shut the door and seated herself behind the desk, pointing to an orange easy chair across from her.

I discreetly suppressed a shudder at the chair covered in dog hair, perching on a barstool against the wall instead.

She crossed her arms over her flat chest and studied me coolly.

My nervous smile wasn't entirely fake. "Is this is some kind of consultation because I didn't have an appointment—"

"Cut the crap. You're not here for a manicure. What do you want?" From the pack on her desk, she extracted a Pall Mall and placed it between her frosted lips. "The insurance company sent you, didn't they?"

I shrugged. Good a cover as any. I pulled out my own smokes and miniature notebook. She clicked open her silver butane lighter and held the flame across the desk. When that blessed nicotine filled my lungs, I decided it was a pity that so few people bonded over tobacco anymore. "Since you were expecting me, I hope you won't mind answering a few questions?"

"Got one for you first. What's your name?"

"Julie Collins." I waited for her to ask me for a business card, or anything proving my identity. She didn't. Sometimes we're far too trusting in the "fly-over" states.

Cindy Jo exhaled, staring at me through the haze. "Well, Julie Collins, what is it you want to know?"

"According to our information, your husband, JC Bettleyoun disappeared four weeks ago." She nodded. "The police report said he called you on his cell phone on his way to Kansas City."

"Yep. Of course, we had a fight, which was nothin' new."

"I assume you remember what the fight was about?"

She rolled her eyes. "Him and his damn fool idea of becoming a professional fisherman." Leaning back, she blew smoke rings toward the dingy ceiling before facing me again. "You married?"

"Once. A few years back. Didn't work out."

"I hear ya." Her jaw flexed grotesquely as she filled the space with lopsided smoke rings. "Did you ever look across the breakfast table at the man you'd married, wondering what the hell you'd done? Think I would've learned my lesson when I had that exact same thought with my first husband." Cindy Jo chuckled at my surprised expression. "Guess your little report regarding JC's life insurance policy didn't tell you I'd been married before."

"How long ago?"

"Been twenty years since Eddie, that drunken fool, wrapped his Harley around a pine tree. Died instantly. Left me in a helluva bind. I walked away from that life and never looked back." She gestured around the cramped space with something akin to pride. "Built this place on my own and swore I'd never be dependent on any man to take care of me again. That's what attracted me to JC. He wasn't one of those men who wanted a woman as his cook, maid and whore." She snickered. "Hell, most of the time he was doing those things for me."

A spot beyond the door held her attention and I waited.

"When it was good between us, it was perfect. But when it was bad, it was hell on earth. Know what I mean?"

I knew exactly what she meant; I was well versed in hellish relationships, both familial and intimate.

"As long as I kept money in his account he was willing to let me call the shots. Then he got real cocky and secretive last fall. I knew he was up to no good, with his sudden influx of money." She punctuated her displeasure with the end of her cigarette. "I recognized the pattern. I'd lived through drug raids with Eddie and I'm too damn old to do it again."

Confused, I ground out my half-smoked Marlboro. This conversation wasn't helping. In fact, I found myself sympathizing with Cindy Jo. JC was a total loser. She would be better off if he *had* skipped town. However, I doubted my client would be pleased with my analysis. "Do you have any idea where JC is?"

"Dead, probably."

I lifted a brow and leaned back on the stool. Both Rich and Cindy Jo assumed JC was dead.

"I don't play the part of the grieving widow very convincingly, do I?" A frustrated hand raked her glossy hair. "I'll be honest. JC was stupid to get mixed up in the drug trade. If he hadn't disappeared, we'd be in divorce court anyway. I talked to our attorney last week and found out another interesting tidbit. Seems before he took off, he changed his will."

"The lawyer disclosed the new terms of JC's will to you?" I frowned. "Isn't that illegal?"

"Of course. But he knows which side his bread is buttered on."

That description fit a boatload of lawyers, but a greasy one in particular floated to the top in my mind. "Charles LaChance?"

Cindy Jo nodded, unperturbed by my guess.

"Why would JC change his will?"

"Because he was a bastard. After he became flush with cash, he took great joy in telling me he didn't need my money. The real kicker?" Her razor sharp laugh sliced the stale air like her deadly fingernails. "I'm the one who encouraged him to get a fucking hobby. I bought him his first goddamn rod and reel."

Ouch.

"The one thing he had that was worth anything was that ridiculously expensive fishing boat. And he willed it to his fishing buddy, Rich Barber."

The hair on the back of my neck stood up. "Why?"

"Good question. Maybe you should ask Rich."

Oh, I planned to. "Have you told this to the police?"

"Hell, yes. Guess they questioned Rich after I told them about the new development, but they had no reason to hold him, so they let him go."

The lighter in her hand clicked open and shut in a hypnotizing rhythm. "Rich doesn't have a pot to piss in. So, tell me, in your expert opinion. Isn't inheriting a fifty-thousand dollar boat an incentive to make someone disappear?"

Absolutely. Rich Barber had seemed so oddly sincere.

Or was Cindy Jo leading me astray? Another possibility skated through my mind: Were she and Rich in it together?

Before I could comment, the door opened and a pack of furry creatures streaked past my ankles. I picked a hairball off my linen trousers and dropped it onto the shag carpet.

Cindy Jo's face cracked into an enormous grin. She scooped the beribboned beasts onto her lap. "Oh, don't you all look sweet." The animals began jumping up and licking her face in earnest.

When she puckered her lips to accept the enthusiastic doggie kisses, I turned away. Eww. I'd almost rather witness old people doing the nasty than watch this disgusting display of canine affection.

Mandy stood in the doorway, holding out a tiny, apricot colored ball of fluff. "You forgot one," she cooed, rubbing the fuzzy thing under her double chin. "Isn't she just precious? Melanie said she cowered after the bubble bath, but sat regal as a princess for the comb-out and blow dry." Mandy smiled at me and whispered conspiratorially, "She had her first salon appointment today."

"Nice," I mumbled, clueless as to how to respond.

"You ready to do their nails?"

"Yeah. Bring that new fuchsia." Cindy Jo tousled a furry ear. "It's a perfect match for these darling bows."

I leapt up to follow Mandy out the door. My preliminary report to Rich had more questions than answers, and he hadn't paid me nearly enough to watch dogs get a pedicure. Or was it a pet-i-cure? A paw-di-cure? I bit my lip to keep from chortling at my inappropriate sense of humor.

"That's my precious, precious girl," Cindy Jo baby-talked, kissing the top of the dog's head. Her gaze met mine and she proudly gathered her pets to her bosom. "These are my babies. Eeny"—she patted a black head, then pointed to the gray one—"Meeny"—she scratched the ivory chin—"Miny—"

"Suppose that one is Moe," I quipped.

Her mouth flattened into a grim line, her eyes turning as hard as a pumice stone. "No. Moe passed on unexpectedly a few months ago." She focused her attention to the whimpering dog. "This angel was sent to fill that empty space in my heart."

"What is her name?" I asked, trying to make up for stepping in a verbal pile of doggie doo-doo.

"Mignon."

Not such an odd name, considering the fuzz ball was a French poodle, but I was hoping she'd been christened Curly…And people told me watching too much TV would cause my mental muscles to atrophy.

"I won't keep you. I'll check in again, but if you hear from JC, will you let us know?"

Her lips curved into a disbelieving smirk—as if she knew that wasn't a possibility. "Of course."

~*~

Curious about fishing regulations and bow fishing practices in particular, I stopped at the Game, Fish and Parks office to pick up a fishing guide. Usually government handbooks are dry reading, but this information fascinated me.

Who knew there were so many kinds of funky fish in our small state? Northern pike, bourbot, three species of catfish, not to mention the scale-less and creepy, but highly sought after prehistoric paddlefish found only in the Missouri River and its tributaries.

Apparently the Black Hills boasts some of the best trout fishing in the country. Although trout aren't indigenous to the area, streams are stocked with three varieties: rainbow, brown and brook. In the last few years, record breaking walleye had been pulled from the waters of Angostura by amateur anglers. And we were a mere three hour drive from the Missouri River, rumored to contain catfish and pike the size of sharks, if one believed the fish tales passed down as legend.

So why had JC chosen bass fishing? There were few trophy-sized small-mouth bass to be had around here, especially in areas where GF&P mandated a catch and release policy. Tournaments used the combined weight of five fish to determine winners. JC seemed like the macho type who'd prefer something marlin-sized to hang on his wall.

With more questions than answers, I needed a fresh perspective on this situation. Since it was getting late in the day, I checked with the answering service to see if I had any new messages. Nothing. It'd been a boring couple of weeks in the PI biz, so I decided to head home and tackle the case again the following day.

Chapter 2~ Casting the Line

I placed a "Gone Fishing" sign on the office door the next morning and made the hour-long drive south on Highway 79 to Hot Springs. The vast sky spread across the landscape in a brilliant, cloudless blue, the perfect foil for the rolling fields of gold and the dark green pine trees dotting the rocky hills. Not even the red dirt devils blowing over my clean car dimmed my mood. I was out of the office for a change and it felt good.

Angostura Reservoir had been created in the 1940s by trapping the Cheyenne River in a small, sleepy canyon. The man-made lake is surrounded by soft sand beaches, rock and dirt cliffs, and a mix of deciduous and pine trees. The water is warm, considering the elevation, and very clean, fluctuating between murky in the shallow spots and a dazzling silver-aqua where it drops off to seventy-five feet. Once the water trickles back over the dam, the river resumes its natural course.

I'd been camping at the lake at least once a summer during my high school years. The majority of my time had been spent lying on the beach, working on my tan and drinking cheap beer. And if Kevin and I were lucky enough to hook up with people who had a boat, we hadn't spent time messing with poles, lines, bait and the like. We'd cruise around, trying our luck at cliff diving in the restricted area by the dam, and hope like hell the rangers didn't catch us with a cooler full of Coors Light. Nothing more humiliating than having to empty the cooler and pour every drop of beer on the sand because we were underage.

I remembered there were four separate areas to launch and dock boats. Today, the sailboat beach didn't interest me any more than the main dock where Jet Skis, pontoons and other recreational water vehicles were rented at the floating convenience store. Serious fisherman docked at the less fashionable section down from the dam, or on the north side of the lake. Since Rich had mentioned a bait shop, I tried my luck on the north side first.

My flip-flops smacked the blacktop as I walked beneath the shade of big cottonwood trees, bypassing fly-laden garbage cans along the side of the road. The docks were deserted. I counted about thirty boat slips, and noted the location of the red tarp before beginning to look for Rich's boat.

I found it easily, humble machine that it was: wood and aluminum, flat bottomed with a small platform surrounded by three, sad-looking spotlights. I eased onboard, surprised at the stability and unlocked the tiny, homemade compartment below the decking that housed equipment—fishing poles, tackle boxes and, most importantly, the bow, the cabling system, the reel, the chains and the arrows needed for bow fishing.

My fingers stroked the arrow's smooth shaft. I was accustomed to graphite arrows with target or broadhead tips. These arrows were buoyant aluminum, with pre-drilled holes for the cabling system to loop through, attached to a swivel, and then crimped in two places. With my fingertip I followed where the line was tied onto the other end of the swivel, so the tension was not on the line but on the cable, allowing the line to move along the arrow without friction. Pretty cool concept. Especially the reel. Swimming after arrows that had missed their target didn't sound like much fun, and this piece of ingenuity fixed that problem.

The nocks were similar; however, the metal arrow tips were different. Innocuous in the closed position, but once they penetrated the prey, two deadly barbs straightened, preventing the catch from sliding off the arrow. Once the fish had been landed, the arrow tip is turned, releasing the barb back to its straight position to remove the catch from the arrow without resistance. I wouldn't want to pull the arrow back through fish skin, guts and bone.

Killing was messy and for most sportsmen, part of the fun. Not for me. It'd been a few years since I'd made an animal kill. These days I used my bow as a stress reliever, practicing with target tips to keep my hand/eye coordination up to snuff.

As eager as I was to test my skill, first I had to check out JC's boat. I stripped down to my bikini, grabbed a tackle box as cover and sauntered over to slip number twenty-seven. The bait shop had a *Closed* sign, but I never assumed anything.

I unsnapped the tarp and just about threw up from the stench of rotten meat. Jesus. Had he left dead fish or bait decaying someplace? Despite the gag-inducing odors, I scoured the boat from stem to stern, coming up empty-handed on clues as to where JC might've gone or finding Rich's knife.

As I rolled the tarp back into place, a gruff voice demanded, "What in tarnation do you think you're doin'?"

I stood up straight and faced the troll eyeing my butt. He reeked of dead fish and something dank, earthy and foul. Thrusting out my meager chest—most men don't care about breast size when faced with a string bikini top. They only care that cleavage actually spills out. I tossed my hair while producing a smile that rivaled the devil's. "I'm looking for my boyfriend's fillet knife."

He wheezed disbelief, wiping away a string of spittle with his grubby hand. "Nice try. But I happen to know the man that owns this here boat ain't got a girlfriend, and you sure as shootin' ain't his scrawny-ass bitch of a wife. She's been down here all the time this last month."

"Really? I suppose she must be missing him, because he up and disappeared on her. Did she say anything to you about that?"

He snorted. "She's crazy, siccing them yapping damn dogs of hers on me if I show my face anywhere near her. But that still don't tell me why *you're* tryin' to convince me that he's your boyfriend?"

My best spur-of-the-moment plan involved batting my eyelashes and letting loose an embarrassed giggle. "Oh, JC isn't my boyfriend, Rich Barber is my boyfriend. See, I came down here to work on my tan," I spun around, wiggling my backside. "I figured as long as I was down here

I could look for the knife JC borrowed before he took off. Poor Rich has been missing it and I wanted to surprise him by bringing it back tonight."

"Then why did I have to chase your boyfriend away from this here boat just last week?"

Seemed Rich had forgotten to relay that little factoid to me.

"Well?" He crossed his arms over his beer belly and sneered instead of leered.

I opened my mouth but he beat me to the punch.

"Uh-huh. Don't care what your story is, this here boat is private property, now move it before I call the Ranger."

Didn't need to tell me twice.

I replaced the tarp, picked up my tackle box and jiggled back to Rich's boat, knowing the perv was watching my every move. The motor caught on the third try. Once I putted out of the 'no wake zone' I opened the throttle. Or tried to, but Rich's boat lacked horsepower. No wonder he had boat envy.

The question was: Would he kill for it?

I spent the next three hours wrestling lines, reels and the nearly indecipherable cable connections.

Rich's bow was lightweight and shorter than mine. With the extra equipment attached it seemed heavier and infinitely more awkward. Reeling in the spent arrow was time-consuming and cumbersome. I imagined with the drag ratio of the water—if one actually hit a moving target—it wouldn't take long to build some impressive biceps. I was happier practicing shooting at a bale of hay in my backyard while swigging a beer. I was even happier yet to dock the boat, store the equipment, hop in my car and go home.

I wasn't looking forward to telling Rich he'd wasted his three hundred bucks. His suspicions about Cindy Jo—and this case in general—seemed dead in the water.

~*~

On the drive back into town I considered my evening entertainment options after I checked in with the answering service. No word from Kevin. No potential clients needing our expertise. Depressing that my cell phone showed I hadn't missed any calls or texts during my six hours at the lake.

My main squeeze, Martinez, had Hombres business to attend to tonight, so I knew he wouldn't be home until late—if at all. I'd spent enough time alone today and wanted to go out. My usual pals had deserted me. Kevin was gone on a skip-trace—that motherfucker took all the fun cases. Yeah, it gave me an ego boost that Kevin trusted me with the business while he was out of town, but he'd been gone a lot lately, and I missed him.

My pool-playing buddy Jimmer wasn't answering his phone, but I left him a message anyway. My former BFF Kim had become my meet-for-coffee-in-a-kid-friendly-place kind of friend instead of the wild type who'd hole up in a dive bar with me, knocking back tequila shooters until we passed out. I missed those days.

I needed booze. I needed conversation. I probably needed to get my fucking head examined for driving to Fat Bob's, the biker bar Martinez owned. Over the years I'd been banned from the bar, tossed out on my ass into the parking lot, and locked up in the back room. Fun times—none of which I wanted to repeat. So why was I here?

Loneliness.

But I justified my choice; at least I hadn't chosen Bare Assets, the strip club Martinez also owned, because guaranteed I'd get kicked out due to my...issues with the management. And the staff. The strippers kind of liked me however, so there was that. Life was never boring when you're involved with the International President of the Hombres motorcycle club, although Martinez would argue that I caused more than enough trouble on my own. Maybe in the past, but it'd been ages since I'd ripped it up—not that I was looking for trouble tonight.

I barked a mental "fuck off" to the smarmy voice that reminded me every time I went out in this kind of mood, a fight usually found me.

As I turned into Fat Bob's empty parking lot, I wondered if they'd closed for the night. The place was always jammed, even on weeknights. But the neon sign flashed **OPEN.**

Weird.

After parking in my usual spot at the back of the building, I shouldered my purse and hoofed it to the main entrance. No bouncer manned the front door—not even a lowly Hombres pledge. Inside I stopped and stared across the space. A half a dozen people milled around. That was it? Had the cops made a bust? It'd be a first; I'd never seen cops at either of the businesses Martinez owned and I never asked why.

Big Mike had his back to the door as he flipped through channels on a TV screen behind the bar. Huh. I'd never seen anyone turn on that TV; I'd always assumed it was broken.

Reena, the only cocktail waitress I could stand—or rather, who could stand me—jerked her head at Big Mike to get his attention as I approached the bar.

Grinning, he grabbed a bottle of Coors Light out of the cooler, twisted off the lid and meandered over to me. "What's up, trouble?"

I slid onto the barstool and pulled out my smokes. "What makes you think anything is up?"

"Because you never sit at the bar. Especially not alone."

"That's because out here there are too many men trying to get a piece of me. Makes Martinez twitchy and violent, and ain't nothing good ever comes of that."

"You've got a point."

"Anyone lurking in the back office?"

Big Mike shook his head and set the beer in front of me.

"There's your answer as to why I'm gracing you with my presence up front." I held my cigarette out for him to light, which he always did; he was a gentleman that way. I inhaled and blew out a stream of smoke. "Why's it so dead in here tonight?"

"Poker run and a Rob Zombie concert up in Deadwood."

"Hombres providing security for the event?"

He nodded. "So why aren't you hanging and banging the bossman?"

"He had 'shit to do' as he so lovingly informed me this morning."

"Jesus. I thought that meant he was doin' you."

I muttered, "I wish."

Big Mike's eyes narrowed. "You two aren't fighting again?"

"No. In fact, things are going along swimmingly."

"Swimmingly?"

"You know...As in peachy keen. Fine as frog's hair. Two sweet peas in a pod. Happy as fucking clams. All that sappy shit." Which was true for the first time ever in our tumultuous relationship. Part of me waited for the other motorcycle boot to drop and for everything to go to hell. But that was a small part of me.

"I figured as much."

"Why? Did he quit listening to the police scanner for mention of my name or something?"

"You wish. Just because you've been without conflict doesn't mean you won't be in the thick of shootin' up cars or starting bar fights again. Sooner rather than later is my guess."

"Been pretty damn boring all around, hasn't it?"

He laughed. "Maybe that's why things are going along *swimmingly*—you haven't done anything to piss Martinez off or to put yourself in danger."

Now my eyes narrowed. "Speaking of putting himself in danger, why don't *you* know where he is? You're his damn bodyguard."

Big Mike snorted. "I'm *one* of his bodyguards. I also got the same 'shit to do' response you did but, unlike you, I ain't allowed to ask questions. I just do what I'm told, which tonight, is tend bar."

"Who's on duty with him?"

"Cal is handling security for the concert. Buzz is tasked as his personal security. Before you ask, Martinez ain't been in tonight and I don't know if he's coming in."

"Then it's a good thing I wasn't planning on waiting around for him." I knocked back a mouthful of beer.

His gaze moved over my bare arms. "Looks like you got some sun today. Taking time off to play?"

"No. A new case. I actually got to leave the office for a few hours and do some investigating." Although, I still wasn't convinced Rich Barber even had a case, even if JC Bettleyoun was most likely dead. I'd found enough dead bodies—and caught enough hell for it from local law enforcement—that I wouldn't exert myself trying to find the missing man. At some point in the last year my curiosity had become more manageable, which is why I hadn't found trouble recently.

But, as usual, the case got me to thinking about other things. Friends and family crap I'd put out of my mind. Wondering why I wondered—or even cared—whether my father had ever taken my half-siblings fishing, when he'd never taken me.

"Julie? You all right?"

"Yeah." I flicked an ash. "Lemme ask you something. Did you ever go fishing as a kid?"

Big Mike didn't bat an eyelash at my abrupt subject change; he was used to it with me. "A couple times. Never liked it much."

"So you don't have happy family memories where your dad, grandpa, or uncle taught you how to bait a hook and then blathered on about life lessons as you cast a line?"

"Hardly. Last time I went, my pops and grandpops got liquored up, passed out drunk in the boat and I was stuck in the middle of the fuckin' lake for four hours until the assholes sobered up." He cocked his head. "Why? You taking a...*poll*?"

I groaned at his pun. "No, I just don't get the fascination with it. Why some guys like to sit in a damn boat all day surrounded by stinky bait. My partner Kevin likes to fish so much he parks his ass on a frozen lake in the winter," I scoffed. "Who does that shit? Then there's fly fishing. Bow fishing. Sport fishing. I found out that some guys actually get *paid* to fish. That's their fucking job."

Big Mike rested his elbows on the bar. "What's all this got to do with anything? You fishing for information on bossman?"

"Christ, stop with the puns. I'm serious. I had no clue Martinez was an avid snow skier. Does that mean he water skis too? What's to say the man isn't hiding a rod and reel and he's planning to spring that hobby on me?" I sucked in a lungful of smoke and exhaled.

"Worried he'll try and lure you in and you want me to help you tackle the problem?" He laughed when I growled at him. "I'm done baiting you with puns. So what's this really about?"

"Tony's birthday is coming up. I have no fucking idea what to get him." I pointed at Big Mike with my beer bottle. "And no, I wasn't thinking about buying him a bait bucket and a pole. After hearing that some guys have become professional fisherman, it just got me to thinking about when hobbies become jobs. Like my nosiness led Kevin to hiring me part time and now I make a living as a PI. So, did Martinez always love bikes? After he scored his first Harley did he get into it so much that he sought out a motorcycle club and became entrenched in the lifestyle? And now he's international president? He never talks about that."

Big Mike's friendly expression had vanished.

Annoyed, I said, "I'm not asking you for club secrets or specifics on how Martinez came into power. I'm just thinking out loud."

He answered me with silence. Then he grabbed me another beer. Probably to shut me up.

So maybe I had been pumping his bodyguard for information because I wanted to do something special for Martinez' birthday. Even when it wasn't one of the big "number" birthdays that people make such a big deal over with ages emblazoned on coffee mugs, black balloons and headstone-shaped cakes.

"What ideas have you come up with for his birthday, so far? Because he don't like surprises."

"No shit? So jumping out of a gigantic cake wearing nothing but frosting during an Hombres meeting at the clubhouse isn't a good idea?"

Big Mike muttered, "You're such a smartass."

The chair seat next to me whooshed and I turned, startled to see Jimmer. How the hell had I missed his entrance? The guy was ogre-sized and I'd only had one beer.

"Hey little missy. You rang?" He swiped my fresh beer and guzzled it. Setting the empty on the bar, he signaled Big Mike for another.

"Thirsty?" I said sarcastically.

"Yep." Then he belched.

I have such classy friends. Now I was sorry I'd called him.

No, you're not. This man has saved your ass and your sanity on numerous occasions. And he is *here. He's the only one who's here.*

"Where's Martinez?" Jimmer asked.

I shrugged. "We live together, but we don't have a color-coded chart on the fridge listing our whereabouts 24/7."

"Be easier if you did."

Big Mike dropped off two Coors Light bottles before he took Reena's drink order at the other end of the bar.

Now that we were somewhat alone, I said, "So why'd you send Rich Barber to me?"

Jimmer's heavy eyebrows squished together when he frowned. "I didn't send him to you. I sent him to Wells."

"Kevin is out of the office. Which means I dealt with him."

"Fuck. That wasn't supposed to happen. That's why I told him specifically to ask only for Kevin."

"Because you don't think I have the investigating chops to help him since I don't have a dick?" I said sharply.

"Back off on the attitude. You're a bad ass with steel balls, okay? Make you feel better?"

I fired up another cigarette and blew the smoke in his face.

He treated me to his I'll-break-you-like-a-twig-if-you-do-that-again stare and I waved the excess smoke out of his face with a murmured, "Sorry."

"You are helping Rich, aren't you?"

"I said I'd look into his concerns."

Jimmer swigged his beer. "As tough as you think you are, little missy, sometimes you are a soft touch. I sent Rich to *Kevin*," he emphasized, "because Kev would've listened, told him this supposed suspicion had no merit and sent him on his way. But you didn't do that, did you?"

"No. How do you know Rich?"

"Pawn shop. I also know he ain't playing with a full clip."

That seemed harsh. Then again, this was Jimmer. "Did you know his buddy JC that went missing?"

"Yeah. Fuckin' prick. Tried to pawn some shit that wasn't his to pawn. I banned him from the store after that."

Another check mark in the *JC is an asshole* column. "After talking to JC's wife Cindy Jo...she hinted that Rich might've had a hand in JC's disappearance."

Jimmer shook his big head. "The guy ain't smart enough."

"Even when Rich stood to inherit JC's fifty-thousand -dollar fishing boat if something happened to him?"

"Even then." Jimmer got right in my face. "Let it go, Jules. JC hooked up with some bad dudes in the last year and you don't wanna go poking into their business. Martinez won't be happy either, because it puts him in a tricky situation with said bad dudes." He pointed at me with the beer bottle. "Which is yet another reason I had Rich ask for *Kevin*, not you."

Shit. Pride had made me take the case. Would my pride allow me to drop it?

You don't think there is a case, remember?

Still, I'd have to stop over and talk to Rich tomorrow and bow out, now that things had gotten complicated.

"Come on. Let's play some pool. Same ol' rules; shot for shot. Miss a shot and you drink a shot."

I sent him a dubious look.

"You're the one who called me, remember? Said you were lonely and wanted to get your drink on." Jimmer leaned over and looked at my crotch. "Show me them steel balls, little missy." His eyes met mine with a full-on challenge. "Or didja let Martinez borrow them?"

"Fuck that. And fuck you. Rack 'em up."

Julie Collins, Impulsive be thy name.

Big Mike grinned at me and set a bottle of Don Julio tequila on a tray with two shot glasses. "Like I said, if you don't go lookin' for trouble it finds you anyway."

"Now you just jinxed me. Anything that happens is on your head, Big Mike."

"Like that's anything new."

~*~

After laying claim to the primo booth in the back room that unofficially belonged to the Hombres, Jimmer and I played three games of pool. I'd missed a dozen shots, but hadn't knocked back more than eight shots of tequila. Jimmer had six misses, but since he outweighs me by a hundred pounds, he wasn't feeling nearly as loose as I was.

That's when they walked in.

They—meaning three couples in full biker poseur mode. From the looks of it, they'd finished the poker run and hopped up on Harley fumes, decided to stop into Fat Bob's—a "real" biker bar.

Jimmer waited menacingly at the end of the pool table for them to pass by. None of them made eye contact with him.

Or with me for that matter.

Good friend that he is, Jimmer listened to my birthday ideas for my man without too much sarcasm. Before we could get the details squared away, he received a phone call and lit out without so much as a goodbye, leaving me in the company of my good buddy Don Julio.

Within ten minutes of Jimmer's departure, I realized the three couples were eyeing my booth.

Eventually douchebag #1 sent his girlfriend/wife over. The far-too-classy-looking-for-a-skanky-biker-bar brunette scanned me and my half empty bottle of tequila, but couldn't quite conjure up a smile. "Is your boyfriend coming back?"

"He's not my boyfriend."

"Fine. Is your friend coming back?"

"Probably not."

"Then you won't need this much space. Would you mind swapping tables with us?"

"Yes, actually, I would mind." I made a shooing motion at her.

She teetered away on stiletto boots that no real biker chick would be caught dead wearing, especially on the back of a bike.

The group conferred. I smoked. It seemed instead of having a good time where they were, they were more interested in booting my ass out of the booth and having a better time over here.

Yeah, good luck with that, motherfuckers.

A tiny blonde, around my age, proud of her big rack from the obvious way she displayed it, sauntered over. Up close she was one of those flawless makeup, perfect hair types. She checked out my sunburned skin, windblown hair, sleeveless T-shirt, jean capris and rhinestone flip-flops.

Instead of a sneer, she smiled. "I'd offer to arm wrestle you for this booth, but there's a wild look about you that guarantees I'll get beat. So how about this?" She placed her palms flat on the table. "See the guy in the leather jacket with the black and gray scruff?"

My eyes cut in that direction. Tall guy. Skinny. Probably fifty. Not bad looking. I'd guess a white-collar guy dressing down to blend in. "What about him?"

"He's my date. I just met his friends a few hours ago and tonight has sucked ass. The guys talk amongst themselves and the wives are snarky when they're not ignoring me completely. It'd help me out a lot of if you'd share your booth."

"Why should I help you out?"

"Because ever since your friend left, you look as if you don't wanna hang out by yourself, and I don't wanna hang out with them. Plus, you look more like my type of person anyway."

"What type is that?"

"The fun, shootin' tequila type that doesn't take any shit from anyone."

I ground out my cigarette, just buzzed enough that her flattery hit right on the mark. Hadn't I recently lamented about my lack of friends? "Now that you mention it, I *am* low on drinking buddies. What's your name?"

"Lisa Morgan. Yours?"

"Julie Collins."

"Well, Julie, what do you say?"

"I say have a seat. But be warned. Maybe I'm by myself because I'm an asshole."

Lisa laughed. "I'll take my chances." She motioned the rest of her party to come over. The women each gave me a polite lip twitch that sort of resembled a smile. I didn't bother learning any of their names, nor did I offer to share my bottle of Don Julio.

I felt Big Mike's eyes on me. He sent Reena over. No one but Lisa noticed that Reena addressed me because they were all too busy barking drink orders at her.

My new friend scrutinized me and I bristled. "What?"

"Who are you?"

"What do you mean?" I poured myself another shot.

"First the enormous guy playing pool with you would've happily whacked any of us with his cue if we dared approach you. Then there's your 'fuck off this is my turf' attitude while you're knocking back a hundred dollar bottle of tequila. Now the bartender, another giant dude, keeps glowering over here. And the cocktail waitress nearly bowed before you. So what gives?" Lisa turned her back to her friends and upended my shot of tequila.

Damn. I liked this bitch. I poured another shot and put it out of her reach as I lit a Marlboro. "I'm a regular here."

"I get that." Lisa eyed my smokes.

"Want one?"

She shook her head. "I quit a decade ago. I miss it only when I'm out drinking."

"I've never managed to quit for more than a day. Never wanted to." My gaze caught on the two jabbering women on the other side of the booth, barely pausing to stop for breath, except to wrinkle their noses when cigarette smoke wafted in their direction.

The brunette aimed a brittle smile at me. "Isn't smoking illegal in all bars and restaurants in South Dakota?"

"Probably. But Fat Bob's patrons make their own rules. You really think if the cops show up here they'll be arresting people for *smoking* violations?" I laughed and blew smoke rings at her until she broke eye contact.

Reena dropped off a round. Blended margaritas for the chatterboxes—who the fuck ordered a frozen frou-frou drink in a joint like this? The guys, spread around the pool table, drank beer. Reena left us with two bottles of Coors Light.

"What's your story?" I asked Lisa.

"I'm a medical records administrator for a physicians group. Jeff"—she pointed to her date—"is a pharmaceutical sales rep. I've been divorced long enough that I was starting to miss having a man in my life. Jeff asked me out. I said no...Until I didn't. This is our third date."

"Will there be a fourth?"

Lisa shrugged. "He's nice enough. But he's another one of those 'love me; love my friends' kind of guys. Know what I mean?"

I glanced over at Big Mike. I'd spent more time with him than any of Martinez' other bodyguards. He and I had a friendship of sorts. But I never let myself forget that his loyalty wasn't to me and never would be—unless Martinez demanded it. "Yeah, I know what you mean." I exhaled. "He seems a little old for you."

"Guys his age are the sweet spot. Their kids are grown and they're trying to reclaim their youth. Guys my age are usually divorced with joint custody schedules and/or child support payments. Guys younger than me are fun for a while, but lots of them are looking for a baby mama, and that ain't for me."

"No kids for you?"

"Nope. My ex thought I'd change my mind. When I didn't he bailed." Lisa sipped her beer. "What about you?"

"Not interested in adding them to my life either."

"We are soul sistas. I knew there was a reason I was drawn to you. Now if you tell me you love Thai food, romantic comedies and 1970s soul music, I'm officially asking you to be my new BFF."

I laughed. "Better hold off on making those braided friendship bracelets. I'm more of an action flick kind of chick. But I do own Earth, Wind and Fire's greatest hits."

Lisa clinked her bottle to mine. "Close enough."

It felt...good talking to her. I couldn't remember the last time I'd had a conversation with a woman who wasn't a client.

After expanding our conversation to our favorite movies, TV shows, and food, she said, "Is there a man in your life?"

"The guy who owns this place is my boyfriend, my live-in, my old man—whatever the correct term is."

"He's a biker?" she asked cautiously.

It was tempting to say *no, he's* the *biker around here*, but I refrained. "Yep."

"Now the bubble around you makes sense."

I shrugged.

"What do you do for a living?"

"I'm a private investigator."

A pause. "You're pulling my leg."

I dug through my purse until I found a business card and slid it across the table.

Lisa scrutinized it before she looked at me again. "Fuck me. I'm serious about having you as my new BFF because you lead a way more interesting life than I do."

"Not lately." I poured another shot for myself and sipped. "My business partner is doing the dangerous, fun stuff leaving me to handle the mundane aspects. Which is ninety percent of the job."

"Lady, you don't know mundane."

We compared notes on job duties and I conceded that her office work was more tedious than mine. Our laughter somehow prompted her date Jeff to interrupt, cutting short our getting to know each other time.

I excused myself to use the bathroom, debating on whether to use the nicer facilities in Martinez' private office suite. But I suspected afterward I'd crawl between his 1000 thread-count sheets and sack out due to my slightly inebriated state.

Big Mike beckoned me over after I exited the ladies room in the bar, but I waved him off. I paused before heading to the back booth, noticing that the sextet had completely overtaken my space. My eyes narrowed. Fuckers were dead if they were swilling my tequila. When I saw no sign of the bottle, I assumed Reena had picked it up. As I watched them interact, it wasn't that they'd encroached on my space that had me feeling melancholy, but they'd coupled up. If I returned I'd be a seventh wheel.

Nothing new about that.

I backtracked to the juke box. I'd never spent enough time at the front of the bar to peruse the music selection. Pretty much solid biker tunes: ZZ Top, Skynyrd, CCR, Neil Young, The Rolling Stones and a multitude of one-hit wonder bands from the 70s. In other words; all crap.

I'd just decided none of this music was worth even a lousy quarter, when I felt him move in behind me. His hard body. His soft lips on the back of my head. I closed my eyes and breathed him in. Leather. Motorcycle exhaust. The heated scent of his skin.

The man had the uncanny ability to appear when I needed him.

Martinez placed his hands on my hips and buried his face in my hair. He stayed like that for several long moments.

I had to wonder if his show of affection was because the bar was nearly empty and few could witness the softer side of El Presidente.

"Blondie." His raspy voice set little electric charges across my skin, zipping in a line down the back of my body from the nape of my neck to my heels.

Rather than melt against him like I wanted to, I said, "Did Big Mike tattle on me? Because I swear I didn't come into Fat Bob's looking for trouble."

"Trouble seems to find you, regardless."

"Not tonight."

"Happy as I am to hear that, I gotta ask what's going on."

"Why…whatever do you mean?" I didn't simper well and Martinez snorted.

"Why Jimmer called to chew my ass about why you're acting all depressed and shit?"

I spun around and Tony boxed me against the jukebox. Upon seeing his stunning face, I couldn't blame the girly sigh because of too much booze. Even as long as we'd been together I still got that little flip in my stomach when I was this close to him, completely lured in by his looks and his compelling don't-fuck-with-me-vibe. My gaze traveled over his smooth, golden skin, highlighted by the sculpted lines of his cheekbones and strong jaw. His assessing brown eyes could ignite a fire in me or send a shiver of fear straight to my soul. His full lips hid beautiful white teeth that formed the most devastating smile I'd ever seen.

Not that he was smiling at me now.

I slid my hands up his chest and twined my fingers in the mass of silky black hair that brushed his collarbones.

He let me. Another rarity.

Our eyes met. "You're here because you missed me, huh?" I cooed.

"Answer the question."

So much for my sex-kitten act. "I'm not depressed. Just trying to kill some time. Make new friends."

"Why?"

"Why what? Why did Jimmer say I was depressed? Maybe because I called him and complained of boredom, hoping to entice him into hanging out with me, which he did."

"Not that. Why are you trying to make friends in the back room of my bar?"

"Because I don't have any friends at the *front* of your bar?" I joked. Well, half-joked really.

No change in his expression. He just studied me.

And like always, I buckled under the implications of that unblinking stare. "What?"

"What kind of people come into this bar, Julie?"

Lowlifes wasn't an answer I could give him even when we both knew it was true.

"Do those people back there look like the type who hang around in Fat Bob's?"

Don't retort that you wouldn't know since he doesn't let you *hang around either.*

"Don't you find it odd the one night you're in here—alone—that they're chatting you up, trying to establish a friendship with you?"

Stung, I retorted, "You find it so hard to believe that I'm interesting enough that normal people outside of your biker universe want to get to know me?"

"That's exactly what I'm saying," he said evenly. "I don't think they're interested in you as much as they're interested in the elusive woman who shares my bed every night."

"I am not your dirty little secret."

No confirmation or denial from him.

Un. Real. I wanted to shove him away from me, but A) I knew he wouldn't budge even if I used both hands, and B) He was El Presidente, and even when I was pissed off, I had too much respect for his position to disrespect him in his own bar.

I let my hands fall away from him. "Back off."

"No."

I glanced at him from beneath lowered lashes.

"Don't look at me like that," he said softly.

"Like what?"

"Defeated. Cowed. You've never backed down from a fight—with me or anyone else—a day in your life."

"Ironic isn't it? That I'm on my best behavior when I go to your precious bar. I didn't come here trying to lure you away from the *shit to do* you mentioned this morning. I'm not looking to get into trouble, or start a fight, but I still end up in one. But it's worse because it's with you."

"Julie."

Whiny girl had taken control. "Let me go."

"No." Then his rough-skinned fingers curled around my jaw and he tipped my face up.

I opened my mouth to protest his manhandling of me, and he kissed me.

Tony Martinez kissed the living hell out of me.

In public. In his bar.

He made that warning growl when I tugged him closer by his vest. But I needed something to hold onto; the man's kiss had a kick more potent than a bottle of tequila.

After he completely destroyed my composure, he broke the seal of our mouths and dragged his damp lips to my ear. "I don't want to fight with you."

I wanted to angle my head so he could start those long, hot kisses down my throat. "So don't. You started it."

"And I'm gonna end it."

"Sounds promising."

"You still wearing that bikini you put on this morning?" he murmured against my neck.

"You'll have to strip me to find out."

"Deal." He smiled against my cheek. Then he backed off and did another strange thing; he draped his arm over my shoulder, very clearly marking me as taken. And as his. "I'll tell Mike we're headed to the back."

Buzz tipped his chin at me in acknowledgment from the bar. Big Mike smirked about Martinez' PDA, but didn't make a smart comment.

Halfway to the door, Lisa intercepted us. "Hey, Julie. I wondered where you'd disappeared to."

Did it make me more suspicious that Lisa barely gave Martinez a glance? Because few women, okay *no* women, look at me when they could be looking at him.

My brain was just muddled enough to think she'd played it too cool. "Like I had a choice but to bail, after you guys completely took over my booth when I stepped away for a few minutes." I threaded my fingers through Tony's. "I found something better to do anyway."

Lisa's eyes widened. Her gaze moved between Martinez and me, eying his vest and the bulge in his tattooed bicep as he kept a proprietary arm around me. "Can't say as I blame you. It was fun hanging out. Maybe we'll run into each other again sometime."

It was on the tip of my tongue to say I'd like that, but I didn't need to give Martinez an opening to warn her off. I mumbled something like, "See you," and sensed her disappointment when Tony led me away.

Holding my hand, he stopped at the door that kept the back of the building off limits. He punched in the code and once we were on the other side, we waited until the system rearmed. The backroom held shelves with the usual bar supplies including liquor, as well as walk in coolers for the kegs. But the biggest chunk of the space was devoted to Martinez' office suite. He had offices in every place he owned including our house. Overkill? Not when I considered the type of business he was involved in and the danger to a man of his position. I liked the fact he had several fortified hidey-holes he could bolt into if need be.

After decoding yet another door, we passed through the short entryway leading into the suite.

Martinez didn't stop in the living area; he towed me straight into the bedroom.

I wandered to the edge of the bed and waited while he shut and locked the door. As usual I didn't have to wait long.

The hard wall of his chest pressed into my back, his hips were snug against my ass, and his breath stirred my hair. Then those warm, damp lips trailed over the section of skin beneath my earlobe, eliciting my shiver and my soft plea. "Yes. Keep going."

"You undo me, blondie. The way you respond to me. Every. Single. Time."

I didn't have to tell him it'd never been like this with anyone else. That he was it for me. Even through our past struggles and my awareness this would never be an easy, normal relationship, I'd deal with it all as long as I could call him mine. "Tony—"

"Tell me," he urged, alternating soft bites and tender kisses along the cord straining in my neck, while his fingertips lazily trailed up and down my bare arms.

I loved that he's so greedy with me—physically and emotionally. I turned my head and my mouth grazed his temple. "I love you."

"Never, ever get tired of hearing you say that to me." Martinez paused and his breath fanned across my damp skin in an intimate lovers' caress. "*Te quiero mucho.*"

His shock and gratitude, those words he said only to me, always spoken from the heart, never failed to move me. To empower me. I whispered, "Let me show you."

Then he turned me to face him. He swept my hair aside and slowly slid my purse strap down my shoulder, tossing the bag to the floor. Locking those gorgeous heated brown eyes on mine, he unsnapped the buttons on his vest. He reached over and draped it across the back of the chair. Then he yanked off his white T-shirt.

My heart raced and that familiar feeling of lust rolled through me at seeing his chest, beautifully marked up with scars and tats. I couldn't help it; I licked my lips.

"You can look at me like that anytime," he said with a sexy growl.

"I do look at you like this all the time." I reached out and ran my fingers across the thick black letters of my name tattooed over his heart. Although he'd had the tat done a year ago, it still amazed me this beautiful man cared so much about me that he proudly wore my name on his skin. I used both of my hands to trace the ink decorating the tawny gold flesh, the deep cut of his muscled arms and shoulders.

He wordlessly placed his hand over mine and slid my fingers down the center of his torso, over his abs of steel, to his belt buckle. Martinez angled his head to kiss along my jaw. As soon as his jeans were past his knees I dropped to mine.

My buzz faded and I became drunk on him. His taste. His scent.

His rough need. My fingers sent reverent touches across the hard planes of his body as I worshipped the hard length and the masculine center of him with my mouth.

He demanded more. I gave. Willingly.

Oh so willingly. I loved making him lose control. He went wild, bucking his hips, letting the storm of release I'd given him overtake him completely.

In the aftermath, I licked my lips again.

Tony's hand was still twisted in my hair as I brushed my mouth over his thigh just to feel it tremble beneath my lips. I'd earned those thickly muttered Spanish phrases and his soft grunts of satisfaction, so I didn't try to hide my smile.

My gloating didn't last long. Martinez hauled me to my feet, stripped me out of my shirt and capris. He tugged on the strings of my bikini bottoms and they hit the carpet.

Then he tempered the intensity that always exploded between us, showing me his playful, teasing side by using the strings on my bikini top to tie up and immobilize my hands, before he pinned me to the mattress.

When I started to protest, he kissed me to shut me up. And as soon as his lips abandoned mine and zigzagged to all my hot spots, I forgot what the hell I'd intended to complain about.

After he'd made me quake beneath his exacting hands and skillful mouth, Martinez levered himself over me. His dark eyes gauged my every stuttered breath, my every anticipatory tremble as his body powered into mine.

Immediately the heat between us flared again. But he purposely pulled back. Watching me. Dragging out this pleasure for both of us.

I traced the upper bow of his damp lip with my thumb. "I like it like this."

"No, you need it like this." Martinez melted me with his cocky smile right before he lowered his mouth and kissed me in that slow, drugging way I craved.

Every drawn out stroke, every lingering touch, every whispered word against my skin tightened our connection.

When I couldn't hold off any longer and arched into him, he swallowed my cry—his name on my lips a benediction as I unraveled. Then, with my hands gripping his ass and my mouth on his ear, he slammed into me several more glorious times and followed me over the edge.

I zoned out and didn't come to until Martinez rolled to his back and tucked me into his side.

Sated, I settled in and pulled the sheet over us.

After a bit, he said, "So what's this needing to find new 'friends' thing about? You have friends."

I knew he wouldn't let it go. I had to try and explain even if it put a dent in my tough girl armor. "It just hit me that I don't have a girlfriend to hang out with since Kim became a mom. It wouldn't be a big thing, except Kevin's gone most of the time, you're busy running three businesses and the Hombres, and Jimmer doesn't believe in making plans. I thought it'd be nice to have someone to do stuff with."

"What kind of stuff?"

I tossed out an arbitrary girl thing. "Shoe shopping."

"Shoe shopping? Really? That's it?"

My fingers idly traced the curve of his ribcage. "I've pretty much always hung out with guys, so it was fun doing girly stuff with Kim. Now she has no interest in being poured into a cab after too many two-for-one margarita specials. I miss that."

Tony's breath stirred my hair as he waited for me to continue.

"I spend a lot of time by myself. Usually I'm fine with it. But the last couple of days it's bugged me."

He twisted my hair around his finger. "Does it bug you that we don't have dinner and drinks with other couples? Like you saw with those people that were in the backroom?"

I tried to wrap my head around Tony and I sitting in a restaurant, making small talk with others outside our normal world. "That's not us. Without being a dick, this isn't about you and me, it's just about *me*." I poked him in the chest. "And by the way, piss off for trying to crush the friendship rainbow bridge building between me and Lisa. Ego much? She wasn't trying to get close to me to get dirt on you. She thought I was cool and fun. She's been the first person in a long time who's made me feel that way."

Martinez tugged on my hair to get my attention. "*I* think you're cool and fun."

I rolled my eyes. "You wanna go check out fall shoe styles tomorrow and then we'll stop in that little bistro off of West Main for lunch? Then hit ladies night at the Clock Tower?" I laughed at his panicked look. "I didn't think so. And don't say Corny or Buzz would be happy to go with me. I'm not looking to hang out with your hired muscle any more than I already do. And besides, I *am* a private investigator. If Lisa wasn't who she claimed to be, I could find that out."

"I trust your judgment, Julie. It's my nature to be skeptical. So I tell you what, if you're serious about wanting female companionship, I can introduce you to a couple of the guy's old ladies at the clubhouse."

God. I hated that term "old lady" even if it was the only respected term for women on the periphery of the motorcycle club. "You'd be willing to take me to the clubhouse?" For being the big bad leader of the Hombres, Martinez was all about the business and not the social aspect of the club. Ever since he'd handled the situation with Jackal, the former enforcer, very publicly, very personally, very violently, I don't think his biker brothers-in-arms missed him hanging around, passing down judgment. Cal might be the enforcer now, but everyone knew who the real muscle was—El Presidente.

"Yeah. Margie, Gunner's old lady is a tough bitch. As is Annie, Bucket's old lady. You'd get along with both of them fine."

I bit his pectoral and he laughed.

"Think about it."

"I am thinking about Bucket having an old lady. It's surprising."

"Why?"

"Because Bucket is scary as fuck. He never talks about her." Then again, Bucket didn't talk a whole lot around anyone, not just me. "I know the name Gunner. He's...?"

"Sergeant at Arms. You don't see him because he deals exclusively with Hombres business."

Meaning illegal business. Tony and I had maintained a dividing line: no discussing each other's work, which is why our relationship worked.

It also made zero sense that Tony would think Lisa was trying to get close to me. Because even if she was, say a DEA agent masquerading as an office drone, I knew nothing about Martinez' or the Hombres' business. Nothing. But that might change if I started hanging out in the clubhouse. So I understood what a big gesture he'd just made to me by inviting me even deeper into his world.

I scooted up and kissed him. "Thank you."

"It's been mentioned in passing that I need to spend more time with the members anyway. There's a cookout thing this weekend. It won't be such a chore to attend if you're by my side." He cocked his head in challenge. "Especially if you're wearing—"

"No fucking way, Martinez." I pushed onto my knees. "I'll never wear one of those."

His smirk softened the challenge in his eyes. "Rules are rules, blondie. If you're there under my protection, everyone's gotta know it."

"You've already got one of those 'Property of' vests made for me, don't you?"

"Yep."

Hard to be indignant while also being naked, but I pulled it off.

Or thought I did until Tony wrapped his hands around my hips and pulled me on top of him. "It's just a vest. I'm not requiring you to get a 'Property of' tattoo."

"But even if did get a tat I'd still have to wear the damn vest."

"Unless you got the tat on your ass and opted to wear chaps so everyone could see it." He laughed—a real gut buster at my look of horror.

"Not even remotely funny, Martinez."

"Just wear the vest, okay?" His bout of hilarity fled when he framed my face in his hands. "You're the first and only woman who's ever worn my patch. That means something to me, even if it doesn't to you."

That's when I knew, despite my misgivings, despite my inner feminist howling at the very idea of being considered a man's *property*, that I would wear the vest. If not with pride, at least with the knowledge that Martinez belonged to me as much as I belonged to him.

I leaned closer. "Fine. I'll wear it. But only to club events and only if you also buy me a pair of killer leather pants. And kick ass boots."

His smile was a thing of beauty. "Done."

"So should we get dressed and go home?"

"Let's stay here tonight." He pressed a kiss on the top of my breast. "I like you naked. And close by me."

"Yeah, well, I wouldn't kick you out of bed either."

"Good to know." Tony reached for the remote on the nightstand and tucked me into his side. "You wanna watch TV?"

"As long as it's not something on *The History Channel.*"

He flipped through the five million sports channels and paused briefly on one where guys wearing stupid-looking camo/safari clothing were casting a line. "Why'd you grill Big Mike about fishing tonight?"

Of course Big Mike reported everything we discussed to him. "Has to do with a case I am—or was—working on. Just wondered if you were secretly into some type of fishing."

"Only if I hit a fish with my ski when I'm waterskiing."

"So you waterski?"

"I haven't for a while. But after seeing you in a bikini I'm thinking about buying a boat."

I smiled.

The rough tips of Martinez' fingers glided up and down my spine. We'd had pockets of this normalcy in our relationship in the last six months and after all we'd been through to be together, I'd never take it for granted.

I'd started to drift off; the sounds of a ballgame had lulled me into a peaceful state.

Martinez kissed the top of my head and murmured, "You have friends,

Julie. Maybe they won't go shoe shopping with you, but they'd kill for you and bleed for you. But more than that, they'll be there for you without question. Without you even having to ask."

If I wasn't so sleepy, I might've gotten teary eyed at Martinez' reminder of what I already had, and that I shouldn't take it for granted either.

Chapter 3~ Reeling in the Catch

After treating me to the best wake up ever—morning shower sex revs me up better than a triple shot of espresso—Martinez bought me breakfast before we went our separate ways.

I stopped at the office first to get Rich's home address since I'd forgotten to put it the information in my phone. I'll admit I was hoping to see Kevin, our communication was sporadic when he was on assignment. But I noticed he'd dumped his bag of tricks for dealing with a skip trace: arm and leg restraints, cloth and ball gags, a bottle of Febreze, several containers of pepper spray, a pair of sweatpants for those perps he picked up in their birthday suits—that happened more often than one might think—a Taser and a stun gun. After being away for a week, he'd probably just gone home and crashed. But I saw he'd signed off on my weekly case update memo. It reminded me that I hadn't updated case information for Rich Barber and the only thing in his file was the contract. Now that I was dropping the case, I could fill in all the blanks after I spoke to him.

While I was in my office I took the time to do a little online research. For shits and giggles I ran a check on Lisa Morgan. She was exactly who she said she was.

In your face, Martinez.

Maybe I *would* call her for lunch.

I killed time creating invoices listing billable hours for our two biggest clients. And then, not able to put it off any longer I got in the car and drove over to talk to Rich Barber.

Rich lived on the north side of Rapid, in an area of town heavily populated by transients and Native Americans, an area seriously lacking a Neighborhood Watch program.

So when I pulled up in front of his place, the well-kept lawn surprised me, as did the bright red geraniums in the window boxes. I'd run a check on him and knew he didn't have a wife, or a live-in or a roommate, so the spiffed up house with the new paintjob was all his doing. The six-foot high privacy fence surrounding the cracker box house didn't surprise me either.

I wandered up to the front door and rang the doorbell and waited patiently.

No answer.

The morning newspaper spilled out as I opened the screen to knock on the door. I waited a minute or so and then rapped more insistently. No response. Finally, I stood on tiptoe and peeked in the small window inset in the door, but I couldn't see anything through the plastic blinds.

Rich had mentioned he worked the four to midnight shift as a janitor, so I knew he wasn't at work. Maybe he'd picked up an extra shift? I'd peek in his garage windows and see if his car was gone.

Just leave, Julie. Call him and explain. There's no reason you have to do this in person.

But of course, I told the voice of reason to take a hike.

A cracked sidewalk snaked around the backside of the house beneath a row of scraggly lilac bushes. I followed the buckled concrete to the gate between the fence and the garage. I pushed the latch and stepped into the backyard.

I froze.

The back door to the house stood wide open.

In this neighborhood? Not a good sign.

A chill swept up my spine despite the heat of the late morning.

I glanced past the neatly mown yard to the oversized, detached garage. No lights shone and the door was firmly shut and padlocked. So why would Rich have left the house wide open?

He wouldn't have.

My heart rate tripled as I approached the back door.

"Rich?" I yelled over the threshold. "It's Julie Collins. Can I come in?"

No answer.

The door squeaked as I pushed it open another few inches. "Rich?"

I debated about whether to walk in, but when I heard the determined buzzing of flies—hundreds of flies—I forced my feet to move.

Probably should've called the police first; I'd been in a situation like this before. But I followed my instincts, wending my way through the trash-packed house that could've been featured on the TV show *Hoarders.*

Maybe the flies were due to the stacks of garbage. Maybe it's not what you think.

That's when the putrid smell hit me.

I followed my nose and ended up in the bathroom.

It was exactly what I'd thought. My bad feelings had been justified.

Rich was in the tub. Unseeing eyes staring blankly at the yellowed ceiling, his mouth open in a silent scream, flies buzzing in and around his body.

I pinched my nose against the stench and covered my mouth against the bile rising in my throat.

The water in the tub had turned the hideous color of raspberry Kool-Aid. Rich's once lanky frame was bloated. His left arm hung limply on the faded yellow bathmat next to an empty bottle of Everclear. Deep gouges ran from his wrist to his elbow. My gaze moved up to the left side of his neck, caked in rivulets of dried black blood. His carotid artery had been sliced too.

I looked away, not wanting to bear witness to Rich's final indignity, but the glint of steel perched on the edge of the tub caught my attention.

I guess Rich had found his knife after all.

Or someone else had.

~*~

After puking in the lilac bushes and then pulling myself together, I called the police.

Didn't take long for them to arrive—six cop cars with sirens screaming pulled up less than ten minutes later.

I'd specifically requested Detective Mitch Jones, even though I'd hoped to never see him again—I was sure he felt the same way about me—but he was first one on scene.

Perched on the curb, I smoked several cigarettes while the cops did their thing inside. A fire truck showed up—for what I had no clue. I played the waiting game, lost in a fog of shock that was all too familiar to me, waiting for my anger to arise, but all I could feel now was sorrow.

My cell phone remained in my hand—unused as per the detective's orders although I had managed to send Kevin a quick text about what'd gone down—and a cop kept watch on me, and the neighbors gathering in the street.

"Miz Collins?" a male voice said behind me.

"Yes?"

"Detective Jones wants to speak to you."

I stood and followed the cop to the backyard. I glanced briefly at the house and shivered. Since I could see the ambulance backed up in the alley, I knew Rich's body was still inside. The horror of that scene would stay with me forever.

Mitch Jones approached me, his mouth set in a firm line. We'd crossed paths several times. While he didn't treat me like a suspect, he didn't ask if I was all right after discovering someone dead and puffed up like a marshmallow. Without preamble he launched in with, "Let's start from the top."

I gave him the basics and awaited his response.

He finished writing in his tiny notebook and looked at me. "Did he seem depressed or suicidal that last time you spoke to him?"

"Not at all." My gaze flitted over his shoulder to the cops milling around the back door. "Are you calling this a suicide?"

Detective Jones sent me a sharp look. "We're not commenting on the manner of death. That's the ME's job."

"Right." I didn't believe Rich had committed suicide.

At my vague response, I had to suffer through the Detective Jones' lengthy lecture about the job responsibility of private detectives versus cops...blah, blah, blah. I tuned him out and my mind raced to other matters.

What had initially seemed like a joke case had turned into a murder case. I broke it down piece by piece. The one thing that stuck out for me, having seen the crime scene, was the exact and obvious placement of the knife on the edge of the bathtub.

If Rich had sliced open his arm and his neck, could he have been able to set the knife out in plain view? Especially since he would have been bleeding profusely? If those were self-inflicted wounds, it seems more likely that the knife would have fallen into the tub. Or onto the bathmat.

And, how could the knife that Rich claimed was missing, turn up when JC—also missing—was the last person who'd had it?

Maybe JC had taken it home?

My mind flashed to the cuts on Cindy Jo's hands and Rich's warning about the extreme sharpness of his knife.

Maybe JC had it on his person when the drug running "bad dudes" I'd been warned about tracked JC down and took it as a trophy. When they found out that Rich had hired a private investigator to look into JC's disappearance, possibly the bad dudes paid Rich a visit. And Rich had paid with his life.

The truth was, I didn't know any of this for a fact—I was grasping at every available straw and coming up with a straw man.

But one thing was for sure, in either scenario; I'd bet Cindy Jo knew way more than she was telling. Logic dictated either she'd killed Rich herself, or she'd told the bad guys that Rich was digging into something he shouldn't be and they took care of him.

The end result was the same; Rich Barber was dead in what, to me, was supposed to look like a suicide.

Yet I knew one detail the cops hadn't figured out yet. I should've shared the information, but I'd been scolded numerous times in the past by Detective Mitch Jones about not telling the police how to do their jobs. So, I'd leave them to it. Let them figure it out on their own.

I had bigger fish to fry anyway.

~*~

Detective Jones released me and as soon as I was enclosed in the privacy of my car, I made a call.

"Hot Tips, this is Mandy. How can I help y'all?"

"Mandy. It's Julie Collins. I met with Cindy Jo the other day?"

"Oh, you. The one with the slashed up hands. What can I do for you?"

"Cindy Jo and I got to talking and I never did get my manicure. Does she have any openings today?"

"'Fraid not, hon. It's her regular day off."

"Oh. Shoot. She works so hard and I know she's so stressed out about JC being missing that I hope she's doing something fun." *Come on Mandy, take the bait.*

"I don't know how much fun it is for her, but she said she was headed down to Angostura to clean out JC's boat. I think it makes her feel closer to him or something, because she's been doin' that a lot since he went missing."

"The poor thing." It hurt to choke those words out. "I imagine she took her babies with her?"

"Not this time. She dropped them off here at the salon about an hour ago."

Mental high five. "That's awfully thoughtful of you, Mandy, taking care of her doggies for her."

"It's no trouble. They're part of the family. Would you like me to schedule you for an appointment tomorrow?"

"That'd be great," I lied. "The earlier the better."

"Gotcha down at ten a.m."

"Thanks. Bye now." I hung up.

On autopilot, I zipped down Highway 79 toward Angostura. With the images of Rich Barber's dead and bloated body on a flash and repeat circuit in my thoughts, all I could focus on was wondering if my cavalier attitude—not taking his warning about Cindy Jo seriously—had gotten a man murdered.

Before I knew it, I'd reached the north side boat ramp. With Rich's boat key in one hand and my cell phone tucked in the back pocket of my capris, I boarded Rich's boat. Sheer luck or not, the motor sputtered to life on the first try.

Angostura has a reputation for frequent, unexpected gusts of wind. Today was no exception; the gentle breeze turned harsh, whipping the water into a frothy mass of whitecaps. Cold spray stung my face as I pushed the gutless boat to its limit. I hadn't seen another soul since I'd left the dock.

Then I saw JC's red boat bobbing in the water like a lone cherry in a punchbowl.

A small figure stood on the prow.

Somehow seeing Cindy Jo in the flesh jarred the logic center of my brain. What the hell had I been thinking coming down here half-cocked? I realized not only was I alone, I was unarmed, and no one knew I was here. I'd broken the most basic PI rules.

Call Kevin, call Jimmer, call Martinez. Call the damn cops.

I grabbed my cell phone, but it read "no service."

Adrenaline crashed through my system. That, coupled with fear, stirred up an extreme case of nausea.

No time to get seasick, Julie, get your head in the game.

I slowed the boat and hastily rigged up the bow fishing system, praying I'd attached the various lines in the right way. I slid the bow down beside the platform and made my approach.

Cindy Jo actually waved.

Maybe this would be all right.

But as I got closer, I realized she was waving a gun. I didn't care what caliber, type or style of gun she held. It was a gun; a big, shiny gun, and she had it pointed directly at my head.

"Cut the engine and get your hands up where I can see 'em, Julie Collins," she shouted cheerily. "Or I'll blow a hole in you."

I spread my arms wide, every muscle in my body pulled tight as a fisherman's knot.

"I have a bone to pick with you." Her cigarette bobbled in the corner of her mouth as she spoke. "Found out you don't work for the insurance company."

"I never claimed I did," I yelled back, wishing we weren't having this conversation at 100 decibels.

Might as well wish the Ranger would swing by this forgotten cove in his patrol boat and save your dumb butt.

As quickly as the wind blew in, it blew back out, leaving quiet, calm air beneath the gray gloom of the clouds. The lake's surface became as smooth as glass.

Maybe the universe was on my side for a change.

"That's better," Cindy Jo said. "What are you doin' out here, Miss *PI*? Lookin' for clues?"

"Looking for you."

"Why?"

"To find out if you know that Rich Barber is dead."

She grunted and flicked her cigarette butt over the boat rail. It hissed as it hit the water. "So?"

"So. The clues lead to you."

"You got nothin' on me."

"Don't be so sure," I cautioned. "You planted the knife in Rich's bathroom after you killed him."

She gave me her smug attitude. "What makes you think it was me?"

"I didn't at first. I considered the idea that you'd tipped off the mysterious drug guys you kept mentioning—the ones JC might've been working for. Possibly informing them that Rich knew more about what JC had been up to than he'd been letting on, including the bit about Rich hiring me to poke around. I'm pretty sure that'd make guys trying to keep their illegal business on the down low sit up and take notice. But that would bring *you* to their attention. Then I remembered you'd told me you'd had enough of drug dealers with your first husband. Which leads me...back to you. You killed JC. Rich suspected you did it, so you had to kill him, too."

The look on Cindy Jo's face—a mixture of annoyance and admiration—quickly turned arrogant . "Bad choice, Rich bragging to me that he'd hired you. He called me drunk as a skunk, saying you'd figured out that I'd killed JC." Cindy Jo snorted. "Boy was Rich surprised to see me."

Poor, sweet, stupid Rich. He'd been right to call Cindy Jo a psycho, but wrong to bait her like that. Cindy Jo's confident smirk gave me a new direction. "Trying to make his death look like a suicide was clever."

"I thought so." She smiled prettily.

"Except for one thing." I flashed my teeth at her in a non-smile. "All the wounds are on the left side of Rich's body—those vicious slash marks on his left arm and the nick in his carotid on the left side of his neck."

"So?" she said again.

"Rich Barber is left handed. The marks on his body should've been on the right side, not the left. Once the cops figure that out they'll know it was murder, not suicide."

She stared at me dumbfounded and then she snapped, "This whole thing has turned into a goddamned mess."

The boat caught a gentle swell and I slipped toward the loaded bow, still several feet away. "What whole thing?"

Cindy Jo didn't answer immediately. "After you left my office I realized I hadn't checked with our insurance company about the policy on this boat—I didn't want to seem too eager. I already knew since my name wasn't on the title, there was no way I could *sell* the damn thing. But I also knew Rich's name wasn't on the title yet either. I figured I could sink the stupid boat and claim it was an accident, so I'd collect some cash for all my trouble, right?" Her chilling laugh echoed across the water. "Wrong. JC never took out a policy. On a fifty-thousand dollar boat. *What* a moron."

"Where is JC now?"

She angled her chin over her shoulder toward a blue cooler, roughly the size of a portable meat locker, at the back of the boat. "The last of him is in there"—she grinned manically—"in pieces."

My jaw dropped even as my stomach lodged in my throat. "You killed him? Over a fishing boat?"

"Don't be stupid," she sneered. "It was never about the damn boat. I killed him because he skinned and tortured my dog."

"What?"

"JC killed my poodle, Moe. I told him to get rid of the boat or I'd call the cops and turn him in for drug dealing. Believe me, I did it before with my first husband. You bet your ass JC changed his tune PDQ—at least on the outside. He acted all sweet and sorry, cookin' meals, cleanin' house, takin' care of me, especially when Moe went missing. But on the inside he was scheming like a son-of-a-bitch."

I pretended to lose my footing on a rough wave and slid closer to my weapon. Luckily, Cindy Jo didn't appear to notice.

"Moe hadn't gone missing. He killed her." Her eyes turned a flat, lifeless brown. "Truth was, that sick bastard carved up my dog, my beloved baby, and literally fed her to me on a silver platter. I didn't know it wasn't grilled chicken until he gave me that mean little laugh, the one he saved for when he'd pulled something over on me." A sob left her throat, the hand holding the gun wavered. "Then he informed me, in that cocky tone, he was done taking orders. The time had come to *fish or cut bait*."

My confusion was apparent because she clarified, "It's some stupid fisherman's saying. He was leaving me. I didn't care about that, but he wasn't getting away with killing my dog. So I acted fast and decided *he'd* become one with the damn fish he loved so much. As bait."

"How did you...?" I'd become so grossed out by the idea of JC's body parts in the cooler, not to mention grilled poodle steaks, that I couldn't even finish my thought, let alone form a coherent sentence.

"Chop him into bits?" Cindy Jo asked. "My daddy was a rancher. Taught me once you take the head off something, it's just meat from the neck on down." She frowned briefly at the cuts on her palm. "I was pretty rusty. Been a long time since I'd done any butchering. Ended up slicing myself."

My stomach roiled but I snapped back to attention. No way did I want to become another one of Cindy Jo's fillets. "Weren't you afraid you'd get caught dumping his body?"

She looked at me as if I had air bubbles in my head. "I've been bringing JC out here a few pieces at a time. Minus the heart and liver. Those I fed to the dogs. Appropriate, don't you think? Since he proved himself to be a heartless, lily-livered bastard?"

Keep her talking. There has to be another boat around here.

I managed to hook my foot under the bow without tangling the line. The second Cindy Jo got tired of straight-arming that gun at me I'd have her.

"Where is his truck?" I asked.

"I dumped it on the rez. Probably being lived in by a family of five by now." She stared at me thoughtfully. "Nothin' personal, but I have to shoot you. In self-defense, of course."

"They'll never believe you."

"See, that's where you're wrong. I did some checking on you, Miz Collins. Seems you aren't choosy about which men slip between your sheets. No one will question my claim to the cops that JC was running drugs, after you came out here to threaten me to keep my mouth shut because you're doing the Hombres' dirty work. You do know who Tony Martinez is, and what he does, don't you?"

That catty remark about Tony didn't irritate me nearly as much as her comment about the rez. Cindy Jo's attitude was typical of the locals that considered the Indian reservations nothing more than a dumping ground for things—and people—they no longer needed. "I don't deserve to die and neither did Rich."

"Probably not, but JC did use Rich's knife to hack up my baby. I'd planned on putting the rest of JC's pieces in Rich's garage freezer as punishment. See, I figured Rich inheriting the boat was the perfect motive for him to kill JC. The guilt over dicing up his buddy caused him to off himself.

He'd be dead, blamed and I'd be scot-free." A baffled laugh bubbled out. "But I couldn't find the padlock key in Rich's pigsty of a house. So here I am, dropping my chum, JC, across the lake he loved so much."

"No one is going to buy your lame-assed story, Cindy Jo."

"Sure they will. You shot at me, but missed and hit the boat, sinking it." Her eyes gleamed as she built her demented tale. "Fearing for my life, I jumped into the water. I used every ounce of strength to climb into Rich's boat, where we wrestled for the gun. You were caught in the crossfire. It'll be quick, I promise, because I like you. You've got bigger balls than most men." She grinned, leaning closer to the edge. "Still think I'm clever?"

"No."

A wave hit her boat. The gun wobbled and so did she. Before Cindy Jo tried to reclaim her footing, I reached down and scooped up the fishing bow.

Instinctively I settled it at my shoulder, aimed for her chest, pulled back and let the arrow fly. But I hadn't compensated for the drag ratio of the heavier fishing line and the shot veered low, hitting her in the sternum.

The wind masked the sound of metal tearing through flesh, but her shriek of pain echoed loud and clear.

Her arm jerked and the gun dropped overboard with a small splash. She staggered back against the steering column.

I gave one, quick tug on the line and the barbs opened.

Cindy Jo screamed so loud I knew they'd heard it at the docks.

"I wouldn't move if I were you." I pulled on the line eliciting another scream from her. "I can keep doing this until the paramedics get here."

The barbs held. No matter how much she squirmed or flopped around, she wasn't going to be my fish tale—the one that got away.

While keeping a firm grip on the bow, I hunkered down, grabbed my water-logged cell phone. Yes! A clear signal. I dialed 911.

~*~

The rest of the afternoon was a blur of fear, anger and shock.

The Ranger patrol boat arrived first with three Rangers onboard. I handed over the bow attached to Cindy Jo to Ranger #1. Ranger #2 took control of JC's boat and raced to the docks to meet the paramedics. Ranger #3 was stuck with me.

It didn't escape my notice that he was armed. I told him to make note of our location because Cindy Jo's gun was at the bottom of the lake. He said nothing besides telling me to return to the docks. It took a while with the gutless wonder that was Rich's boat.

The ambulance was still there when I pulled into Rich's slip at the dock. Uniforms had swarmed JC's boat. I had a welcoming party waiting for me too: four deputies from the Fall River County Sheriff's Office. After asking my name, they confiscated my phone and my keys. Then they handcuffed me. Out of a sheer case of nerves I made a crack about the cuffs not being the velvet-lined variety I was used to.

No one laughed. They just shoved me in the back of the nearest patrol vehicle.

Shoot one little arrow into a person in self-defense and you're automatically treated like a criminal. How fair was that?

The back of the cop car didn't smell like ass. Probably because the crime rate was so low in this sparsely populated county that the backseat rarely got used. I closed my eyes, but the gruesome images of the day just looped over and over again in my brain, replaying every horrible second. In vivid detail. I allowed myself the tiny bit of comfort knowing that I hadn't been forced to look inside the blue cooler.

The deputy driving me didn't say a word. I didn't ask what would happen to me once we got to the station because I knew. They'd toss me in jail first; ask questions later.

I barely remembered the walk of shame from the cop car to the courthouse, which shared space with the Fall River County jail.

An older woman with an iron grip processed me. I only had to remove my shoes. No hideous prison orange for me.

Still in handcuffs, I shuffled in front of my jailer wearing the disposable slippers they'd issued. I shuddered at hearing the heavy clang of the cell door closing behind me.

On the outside I looked calm, even bored. My response would've shocked the people who knew me. They would've expected me to go in kicking and screaming.

But on the inside? Inside I was curled up in a little ball in the corner, rocking back and forth, scared out of my fucking mind.

Do not shed a single fucking tear.

Do not cause a fucking scene.

Do not threaten to call your fucking lawyer.

Wait it the fuck out.

Since I had the cell to myself, I had all the time in the world to think about what an idiotic thing I'd done—leaving a murder scene to confront a murderer. I'd been so focused on my need for justice that I'd nearly gotten myself killed. To what end? It was only a matter of time before the Rapid City cops would've picked up Cindy Jo.

But she'd almost pitched the last bit of evidence overboard. I stopped her. Who knows if the cops would've gotten to her in time?

Cold comfort as I sat in a jail cell, berating myself over what could've been a much uglier, deadlier situation.

No doubt about it; I'd fucked up.

Hours, days, years seemed to drag on as I waited. After working in the Bear Butte County Sheriff's Office for over three years, I knew the drill. Once they let me out of the containing cell, they'd squirrel me away in an interview room and grill me.

Two hours passed.

Idly, I wondered if they were keeping me this long because they were waiting to see if Cindy Jo died. If that happened this mess would get a whole lot messier.

Finally Sheriff Jim Erickson meandered toward me with a ring of keys. No newfangled keycards for this jail. They were old school all the way.

"Looks like you've had a hell of an interesting day, Julie Collins. You're a long way from Bear Butte County."

I stood. "You remember me?"

"Of course. Sheriff Richards kept hoping you'd apply for a deputy's position up there."

"And here I am, a nosy PI, behind bars."

"Not for long." He inserted the key and the door creaked open. "You ready to answer some questions?"

"I guess." We walked side by side down the hallway. "I take it you've spoken to Detective Jones at the Rapid City PD?"

"Yep." Sheriff Erickson opened the door to a conference room. Two plainclothes cops sat at the table. He unlocked my cuffs and said, "Have a seat." Then he handed me a bottle of water.

"Thanks."

"Start whenever you're ready," he told me.

I needed a cigarette. I'd been in such a hurry to find Cindy Jo that I'd left my smokes in the car. It'd been five hours since my last smoke and my nicotine fit was reaching critical proportions. That's when I noticed one of the detectives had a pack of cigarettes in his front pocket. I leaned forward. "Can I bum a smoke? I won't light up in here, I just need..."

The guy didn't hesitate to feed my addiction since he suffered from the same one.

Feeling the familiarity of the butt between my fingers, and the whiff of tobacco, I calmed down inside. I leaned back and began to speak. "This whole thing started because of a fishing boat."

~*~

Two hours later, my voice was hoarse from answering a nonstop barrage of questions. As far as I could tell, they didn't plan to charge me with skewering Cindy Jo Cracken. I'd done what I had to do in self-defense. I suspected finding bloody chunks of her missing husband in the cooler had helped my case more than anything else.

Finally I was free to go. After receiving my personal belongings from the iron lady—who was much nicer on discharge—I wasn't surprised to discover my cell phone was completely dead. I hated to ask Sheriff Erickson if someone could give me a ride back to my car, but I didn't have a choice.

I turned and faced the sheriff before I walked out into the reception area.

"Something you need, Collins?"

"Yeah. Could someone give me a ride back to the marina? My car is still there."

He frowned at me. "Can't one of your friends give you a lift?"

"Friends?"

He made a shooing motion.

Confused, I waited, facing the door, as the guard buzzed me out of the lockdown area.

As soon as I stepped into the next room, that's when I realized what Sheriff Erickson had meant. I saw Kevin first, then Jimmer, standing near the door.

I remembered Martinez' words from last night. *You have friends, Julie. Maybe they won't go shoe shopping with you, but they'd kill for you and bleed for you. But more than that, they'll be there for you without question. Without you even having to ask.*

Kevin strode forward and wrapped his arms around me.

I sagged into him, knowing he'd hold me up. That was the best part of a decades long friendship; having someone to count on, no matter what.

He sensed I was hanging on by a thread, so he kept our embrace brief and didn't ask me if I was all right. He tilted my head back and gazed into my eyes, concern brimming in his own. "Jules. What can I do?"

"You're doing it by being here." I squeezed him. "I've missed you, partner."

"Same here. I'll have to stick around the office more often just to keep you from getting into trouble."

"Sorry I didn't—"

"Hey. At least you sent me a text. We can talk about the rest of it later, okay?"

"Okay."

He tucked a strand of hair behind my ear, the gesture so casual and familiar I felt tears welling up.

Focus, dammit. No crying now.

I cleared my throat. "How'd you know I was here?"

"Sheriff Richards called and asked if I knew anything about you being involved in a shooting at the lake. Evidently Sheriff Erickson called him. Not two minutes after that Jimmer called. We drove down here together."

"Thanks for being here."

"Always."

The fierceness in his tone reminded me Kevin never had been—or never would be—a fair weather friend.

"Quit hoggin' her," Jimmer complained. Then he enveloped me in a bear hug. "You get yourself into the damndest situations, little missy."

"I know." I whispered, "But like you said, there really wasn't much of a case, was there?"

He smacked me on the ass.

After he set me down, I noticed Big Mike sitting in the waiting room. I scanned the area but didn't see Tony and fought a pang of disappointment. I crossed the room and stood in front of him.

Big Mike smiled but it didn't quite reach his worried eyes. "I won't hug you because bossman might break my arms, but I'm relieved to see you're okay, Julie. Really relieved."

"How did you know I was down here? Did Jimmer or Kevin call Martinez?"

"They were already here when we pulled into the parking lot," Kevin said.

"They?" I repeated to Big Mike.

He pushed to his feet. His big body nearly cast me in shadow. "Do you really think he could stay away when he knew you were in trouble?"

I didn't ask how Martinez knew. The man *always* knew. "Where is he?"

"Waiting outside in the Escalade. You know cop shops ain't his thing."

Kevin snorted and Jimmer elbowed him.

They called after me, but I was already heading out the door.

I had to stop myself from running when I saw him step out of the SUV.

Martinez didn't meet me halfway; he waited for me, his hands closed into angry fists at his sides, those fierce eyes of his cataloguing every inch of me, searching for body trauma that wasn't there—at least not externally.

It hit me all at once. I'd shot someone. While I had no regrets because it had been either her or me, that didn't alter the fact she could die. I'd been in this situation before, not for a while, but it hadn't gotten any easier. And I never wanted it to get easier, either. I never wanted this to happen again, even knowing the odds were high that it would, given the life I led.

I felt the cracks in my fortress of control start to widen and I knew I was in danger of crumbling completely.

That's when Tony strode forward and crushed me against him, staying rock steady, bolstering me before I fell apart.

"It's okay, blondie," he murmured into my hair. "I'm here."

I nodded and found a measure of control. My tears surfaced but never fell, but even if I had started bawling like a baby, Tony wouldn't leave me.

He knew the instant I gathered myself back together. He kissed my forehead. "Now what?"

"Take me home. But first I need to stop someplace and get a pack of cigarettes. I'm dying for a smoke."

He reached into his pocket and pulled out a brand new pack of Marlboros and a book of matches. "Got ya covered."

That nearly set off the waterworks. "God, I love you."

"I know." Martinez' mouth connected with mine in a soft kiss. Then he stared into my eyes. "You'll talk to me about this when we get home? Or do you want Kevin and Jimmer there, too?"

I had a tendency to close down when shit like this went down. Tony wasn't going to let that happen again. "Maybe you'd better invite them over."

"Stay here while I talk to them," he warned, "and suck down a couple of cigarettes because no matter how much trauma and drama you've been through today baby, you're still not ever smoking in my car."

Epilogue~ Or Rather, the Tail End

Cindy Jo lived.

After recovery from her internal injuries, she was charged with first-degree murder in the deaths of JC Bettleyoun and Rich Barber. She pled not guilty by reason of insanity.

She lost the trial. Last I heard she'd fired her lawyer.

Currently, Cindy Jo is trading manicures for cigarettes in the state penitentiary while waiting appeal. For once, I hoped the judicial process would take years.

I don't know what happened to her dogs. Frankly, I don't care. JC did some reprehensible things, but he hadn't deserved to be gutted, filleted and used as fish food.

In a strange twist, animal activists flocked to Cindy Jo's defense. It's a sad world when a dead pampered pooch warrants more sympathy than two dead men.

Once the Rapid City PD released Rich Barber's knife, I returned it to his family, along with the three hundred dollar retainer. They made a token protest, but I insisted. I did come away with Rich's favorite fishing t-shirt, so all was not lost.

Although Rich had inherited the boat, when questions arose about JC's finances regarding the purchase of said boat, Rich's family wisely let the county declare it unclaimed property.

And what happened to the red fishing boat that had wreaked havoc on so many lives? Auctioned by the county. The winning bid? Fifteen thousand dollars. Hopefully, the man who'd purchased it discussed with his wife beforehand.

As the star witness and the hotshot female PI responsible for cracking the case, I suggested the proceeds from the auction of the boat be split between the Boy's and Girl's Club's, to be used for anything *except* a "Teach a Kid to Fish" program.

Of course, they didn't listen to me.

They donated the money to the animal shelter.

Go figure.

~*~

About the Author

The books in **Lori Armstrong's** mystery series have been nominated for and won the Private Eye Writers of America Shamus Award, the WILLA Cather Literary Award, the Daphne du Maurier Award and the High Plains Book Award. SNOW BLIND, the fourth book in the Julie Collins series won the 2008 Shamus Award for Best Paperback Original. The first book in the Mercy Gunderson series, NO MERCY, won the 2010 Shamus Award for Best Hardcover Novel.

Lori also writes contemporary erotic romance as *New York Times* and *USA Today* bestselling author **Lorelei James**. She lives in Rapid City, South Dakota.

Want to connect with Lori? Here's how:

Pop over to Facebook:
www.facebook.com/pages/Lori-Armstrong/420276695091

Join Lori's discussion group on Facebook:
www.facebook.com/groups/LoriArmstrongsOfficialMysteryGroup

Follow Lori on Twitter:
@LoriGArmstrong

Visit Lori's website:
www.loriarmstrong.com

Signup for Lori's newsletter:
www.loriarmstrong.com/Newsletter.php

OTHER TITLES BY THE AUTHOR

Books in the Julie Collins mystery series:

BLOOD TIES

HALLOWED GROUND

SHALLOW GRAVE

SNOW BLIND

Books in the Mercy Gunderson mystery series:

NO MERCY

MERCY KILL

MERCILESS

Coming soon~ THREE SHOTS OF MERCY (collection of Mercy short works)